To

Dr. Robert Michel,
bibliographer of
"McGill in Fiction"
with best wishes
for Christmas and
the New Year

Jan Werpho

27 Nov. 2002

RETURN TO OXFORD

McGill — title, 20

20

59

77

92

118 McGill Daily

160

179 M. gets job m. Gill — 180

climbing towers — 48

meets woman a phase —

? Time — ca. 1968? & was an undergrad in 1950s? (overlaps)
  or later — see mention of Clinton + p. 151 "60s

66 — re friendship ? of women

67ff — transformation ? different hair — 77

"Bill Clayton" 105

theme of orientalists' obsession with oriental woman
  (acad & sexual interests merge)

Return to Oxford

A memoir of a sabbatical year
by Dr Sean O'Malley,
Assistant Professor of Persian,
Institute of Islamic Studies,
McGill University, Montreal,
former Rhodes Scholar, Oxford.

Edited by his friend
Jan Witold Weryho

The Pentland Press Limited
Edinburgh · Cambridge · Durham · USA

First published in 2001 by
The Pentland Press Ltd.
1 Hutton Close
South Church
Bishop Auckland
Durham

British Library Cataloguing in Publication Data.
A catalogue record for this book is available
from the British Library.

ISBN 1 85821 838 1

Typeset by George Wishart & Associates, Whitley Bay.
Printed and bound by Antony Rowe Ltd., Chippenham.

*To the Woman who has inspired
it and who is the model for . . .
With love.*

'I tell you, my friend, it is not good for you to find
you cannot make your dream come true for the
reason that you not strong enough are, or not
clever enough . . . . . . Yes! Very funny this terrible
thing is. A man that is born falls into a dream like
a man who falls into the sea. If he tries to climb
out into the air as inexperienced people endeavour
to do, he drowns – *nicht war?*' (Joseph Conrad.
Lord Jim. Chap. 20)

'How bitter are the regrets of one who has turned
back in his course, only to learn later from
someone else that the road he had set on was the
right one!' (Mircea Eliade. *The Secret of Dr.
Honigberger.* Translated by W.A. Coates. Chap. 7)

FOREWORD

Memoirs of Oxford, fictionalized as well as biographical, are a part of the tradition of the place. There is something about it that tugs at the heart-strings of those who have spent the formative years of their life there. There is too the stimulus of the historical and literary associations of a city which was once hailed as 'Seat of the Muses' and 'the English Athens'. Over 500 novels have been set in Oxford in addition to which are any number of descriptive accounts, some of which have been viewed as literary works in their own right. The reminiscences of *Return to Oxford* can thus be placed within this time-honoured tradition. Like many an Oxford novel, the story concerns a love affair in which the human relationship is coupled with an account of the narrator's relationship with the city. And as is often the case, the movement of the academic year leads from expectation to unexpected developments and finally a sense of closure.

The story concerns the sabbatical year of an Irish-Canadian professor, Dr Sean O'Malley, in the city of his student days. As an outsider and an Orientalist, Jan Weryho's academic casts a dispassionate eye over the 'Englishness' of Oxford. This is accentuated by the exotic nature of the heroine, Morvarid Cama, whose appearance and Zoroastrian background capture O'Malley's heart. The narrative harks back to a time of old-fashioned views and customs through its retrospective gaze, which focuses for the main part on the Oxford of the 1960s but looks back beyond that to the time of the narrator's student days. It is a closed world where university people seldom venture out of the narrow confines of their environment, yet through its romantic interest the story reaches out in scope and geography to embrace the Middle East. At the centre of this Oxford is the Indian Institute, and the college walls here equate to the garden walls of Iran. It is a world imbued with 'otherness' in terms of race, culture and gender. Just as O'Malley struggles to relate to the city, so he faces problems in learning how to relate to Morvarid. As with many an Oxford novel, it is the double narrative that drives the story forward through its interlacing of academic matters with personal romance. In this tale of Orientalism in Oxford, the love affair speaks above all to the powerful attraction of opposites. *Return to Oxford* brings East and West together in the fertile fictional space occupied by the many descendants of Chaucer's Nicholas (*The Miller's Tale*). In a city of walls, where Town once faced Gown, the encounter of a Canadian and an Indian shows that the twain can indeed meet.

John Dougill
Kyoto
12 November 2000

John Dougill is Associate Professor of English Literature at Ryukoku University, Kyoto. He is the author of *Oxford in English Literature* (Ann Arbor, University of Michigan Press, 1998).

CHAPTER I

The taxi turned off Banbury Road into a side street and stopped in front of a house looking very much like its neighbours. I could not see the number across the rainy darkness, but I trusted the driver, who, no doubt expecting a good tip, grabbed my two suitcases, carried them across the little front garden and deposited them on the porch which protected them from the rain. From the joyous tone of his 'Thank you, Sir!' I knew I had not disappointed him. A moment later I heard the sound of his engine departing.

I found myself standing in front of a heavy wooden door. There was a traditional brass knocker in the middle of it, but on the side in the door frame, was the button of an electric bell. I decided to ring the bell, more likely to be heard inside the house.

The door was opened by an Indian woman (at least I thought she was Indian) in a blue sari. Who could she be? Jack Curtis's wife? But Jack had written to me a couple of years ago that he had married an English girl called Joyce. Could he have got divorced and remarried without telling me? People do that sort of thing often nowadays. But the woman was not necessarily an Indian. Some sophisticated Englishwomen like to wear a sari as a form of evening gown. Joyce Curtis, the wife of an Orientalist Oxford don, could very well be one of those.

I had never met Joyce and had no idea what she would look like. The woman standing in front of me had black hair falling

1

on her shoulders. I could not see how white or dark her face was because she was standing with her back to the light. Well, some British people are quite dark, either a throwback to their Celtiberian ancestors, or a more recent admixture of colonial blood. Like Gladys Hungerton in Conan Doyle's *The Lost World*: So dark, 'almost Oriental'. But surely, if Joyce had some Oriental blood, Jack, an enthusiastic Orientalist, would have mentioned it to me.

Then who was this woman? Perhaps a servant? Or have I come to the wrong house? I had trusted my taxi driver to have stopped in front of the right number without looking myself. Those English suburban houses so often look exactly alike. You can find whole streets, even districts of houses all built on the same pattern. I remembered the story of Toby Latham who was an undergraduate in Exeter College during the same years as myself. One late evening he went back to his lodgings after a drinking party. But he entered the wrong house. Front doors were seldom locked in Oxford those days. Toby wisely decided that, after so much booze, he should have something to eat. He easily found his way to the kitchen since all the houses in the street had the same lay-out. He found a loaf of bread and a large sharp knife. The owner of the house was awakened by a strange noise in the kitchen and quietly came down to investigate. Terrified, he phoned the police: 'There is a dangerous-looking burglar with a big knife in my kitchen!' The cops arrived in no time, and the 'burglar', somewhat incongruous in evening dress, was quickly whisked to the police station. The following morning his moral tutor, who happened to be a lawyer, had him cleared of any break-in or attempted burglary charges and quickly released. However he meted out his own punishment to him, not for break-in or burglary, but for excessive drinking leading to a loss of direction. Poor Toby was 'gated' (not permitted out after 9 p.m.) for the rest of the term.

Now, while I did not think I was in danger of arrest, the idea of looking for the right house in the darkness and rain, with two heavy suitcases, my taxi gone, made me shiver.

'Good evening, Ma'am,' I mumbled sheepishly. 'Is this Dr Curtis's house?'

The woman smiled: 'Professor O'Malley? Please come in!'

I felt an immense sense of relief: I was in the right house and I was expected. Jack must have received my letter. I took my suitcases across the threshold and shut the door behind me. The woman extended her hand in greeting, a delicate little hand, so fragile I was afraid to press it too strongly lest I hurt her. But the strangest thing about her hand was a feeling of soothing coolness.

'My name is Morvarid Cama,' the woman introduced herself. From her name I guessed that she was a Parsee. 'I am a tenant and a friend of Jack and Joyce,' she continued. She spoke English with only a slight trace of an Indian intonation, so slight that I might not have noticed it if I had not expected it from her sari-clad appearance.

'Jack and Joyce were going to come back from France yesterday, but they are stuck in Paris Airport because of the strike, you know. Joyce has telephoned and asked me to receive you. I have heard on the wireless' (I noticed she said 'wireless', not 'radio') 'that they are negotiating, and the strike may be over any time. Let us hope they can come back tomorrow.'

I knew all public transportation in France had been paralysed by a general strike. The airports were closed down, the trains were standing still. Of course I was sympathizing with the striking workers, as I always do. Especially when I don't suffer a personal inconvenience from their strike. I didn't know Jack and Joyce had gone to France.

'I am awfully sorry to be causing you so much trouble!' I exclaimed. 'How thoughtless of me! I should have telephoned from London.'

'No trouble at all. It is a pleasure,' answered Ms Cama. Sincerely, or just politely? I wondered. 'Let me show you your room.'

She grasped the handle of one of my two suitcases. My male pride would not allow it. I grabbed it from her before she could lift it. Again our hands met, this time involuntarily. The same soothing coolness.

'Please, Miss Cama!' I exclaimed. 'They are too heavy for a woman! I have books inside them.'

I realized I had called her *Miss* Cama. How did I know she was Miss, not Mrs? I felt pleased she did not correct me.

I carried my two suitcases one by one up the narrow stairs. My room was small, but this was all I needed. I wasn't going to stay long. I didn't want to be a burden on my hosts and intended to look for lodgings soon, preferably in downtown Oxford near the Bodleian and other libraries.

'Please come downstairs after you freshen up,' said my acting hostess. 'You must be hungry after your journey.'

I was eager to accept her invitation. More eager for the company than for the meal. I came down and looked around me. The house had an Oriental decor, as we would expect of the house of an Orientalist don. A large Iranian carpet on the floor and a couple of smaller rugs on the walls. Not the best quality nor the most expensive, I thought, but I am not an authority on carpets. A brass lamp was hanging from the ceiling, spreading its light through a multitude of tiny holes. On the walls hung several Indian and Middle Eastern swords and daggers. Somewhat unexpected in this Oriental museum were a couple of modern abstract paintings. Reproductions of Picasso or Matisse? But they did not look incongruous. I felt the smell of curry coming from the next room.

'I have made the curry very mild,' said my hostess, sounding somewhat apologetic. 'I don't know how you like it.'

'Oh! I love curry!' I exclaimed truthfully. 'But I see you have set the table for one. Aren't you going to join me?'

'I have already eaten, thank you,' she answered quietly.

I felt disappointed. My disappointment was mitigated by the delicious meal, although the curry was a little too mild for my taste. More important, she sat opposite me, very attentive to whatever I might need. 'Could I bring you a cold beer, Professor O'Malley? Jack likes beer with his curry.'

As she sat opposite me I had a better chance to observe her. I thought she looked more Iranian than Indian. The Parsees often claim a pure Persian descent, untinted by Hindu blood. This claim, like all claims of racial purity, has been refuted by anthropologists, including Parsee anthropologists. In the case of my gracious hostess however her Iranian origin was obvious. Her face was dark, but much lighter than the average Indian. Dressed in European clothes she could easily have been taken for an Italian, a Spaniard or even a southern Frenchwoman. Her features likewise looked more Middle Eastern than Indian. Her strong, straight nose made her look not Persian even, but Assyrian. Yes, that was it! She looked more Assyrian than anything, an Assyrian as portrayed in ancient bas-reliefs, or, even more, like one of the many modern Assyrians I had met in the mountains of Kurdistan. I am not an anthropologist, but I am sure there had been a strong Assyrian strain in her Iranian ancestry.

But most impressive were her eyes, dark and deep. Those could not be assigned to any exact geographical location or ethnic group. They were the eyes of the East, found anywhere in the area between Morocco and India. Not of the Far East. East of India the eyes can be as dark and deep and expressive, but their shape is different. The eyes of the so-called 'Middle East' have best been depicted in their full mystery by the ancient Egyptian painters, and no one has surpassed them since. Morvarid Cama's eyes seemed to me like a pair of deep, deep, dark and cool wells greeting a thirsty desert traveller. Yet I could not sustain their hypnotic gaze for long and kept dropping my eyes on my plate. The Baluchi nomads of south-eastern Iran who knew the desert and its dangers had warned me not to look into a dark deep well too long lest I should not resist the temptation to throw myself into it.

I tried to begin a conversation: 'Are you a student, Miss Cama?'

'Yes, I am.'

'Which college?' (In Oxford you always ask a student which college he or she belongs to before asking what does he or she 'read', or study.)

'Lady Margaret Hall.'

'That's convenient. Not far from here. What do you read?'

'English literature.'

'English literature in Oxford! Gee! You have to study Anglo-Saxon and Old Norse and all that stuff?'

'I had to for my BA. I just managed to get through it. I love literature, but I was never interested in linguistics as such. Now it is over, thank God!'

'So you are a postgraduate student. Are you writing a thesis?'

'Yes, I am.'

'What about, may I ask?'

'The Portrayal of the Oriental Woman in Romantic and Victorian Literature.'

'That is a fascinating topic!' I exclaimed. 'You know, it was my teenage reading of Byron and Tom Moore and Kipling and Rider Haggard and Conrad and James Elroy Flecker that had first aroused my interest in the East. And now you, an Oriental woman yourself, must be showing it from a new perspective, hitherto unperceived by Western critics.'

'Oh no! As a literary critic I must not allow my personal background, either as an Oriental or as a woman, to interfere with the objectivity of my study.'

'Judging by your name I take it you are a Parsee?'   *Relig. soot in India – professing Zoroastrianism*

'Yes, I am.'

'From Bombay?'

'Yes.'

'I have never been to Bombay or anywhere in India, but I have met many Zoroastrians in Iran: mostly in Yazd and Kerman, a few in Tehran. Very warm, hospitable people. They drink wine which is forbidden to Muslims. They have a very matter-of-fact attitude towards wine, like the French or the Italians. You should not have too much of it or you will get sick. Too much of any good thing is not good. They do not mystify drink like the British and the Irish, who are apologetic about it, or like the Poles and the Russians, who brag about their drinking powers. In business they have a reputation for honesty, like the Quakers in the West. Many Muslim Iranians have told me they would rather deal with a *Zartoshti* than with a fellow Muslim.'

I could see Miss Cama was pleased to hear my praise of her co-religionists. I continued:

'They were particularly friendly when I told them I was a Christian.' (This was true of modern Iran where they have become a tiny minority. I did not consider it necessary to remind her that before the Arab conquest the Zoroastrian Shahs of the Sassanian dynasty used to persecute Christians. But that was over 1400 years ago!) I continued: 'They even allowed me to visit their fire temples.'

'In India non-Zoroastrians are never permitted to enter a fire temple, said Miss Cama severely. 'I personally do not agree with this rule,' she added apologetically.

'Don't be apologetic,' I answered. 'I think your priests are wise. Kerman, Yazd, even Tehran are out-of-the-way places. But in a cosmopolitan place like Bombay you'd get a crowd of American tourists with flash cameras, not knowing how to show respect in a place of worship of an alien faith; or of their own for that matter. Anyway, the man who particularly impressed me was not formally a Zoroastrian, however much he may have wanted to become one. His name was Ebrahim Pur-e Dawud. He was a professor of ancient Iranian studies in the University of Tehran. I attended his course entitled *'Farhang-e Iran-e Bastan'* (The Culture of Ancient Iran). He was an idealist. He believed Iran needed a moral regeneration which could only be achieved by a return to the ancient principles of 'Good thoughts, good words, good deeds' which, he maintained, have become forgotten with the abandonment of Zoroastrianism. He thought Islam was an alien, Arab religion and its ethic could not take root in the Iranian soul. He regarded this as the cause of the supposed moral emptiness of modern Iran.'

'Did he say all this to a class of Muslim students? How did they take it?' asked Miss Cama incredulously.

'They did not take him seriously. They thought him a harmless eccentric. Nowadays of course it would have been different. A new, very different generation of students has come of age in Iran. Anyway, Professor Pur-e Dawud wanted to convert to the faith of his ancestors. But you people refuse converts, even descendants of Zoroastrians. He went to Bombay, hoping that the English-educated *dastoors* would be more willing to accept him than their Iranian colleagues. No way! Actually the *dastoors* of Tehran had a great respect for his learning and often consulted him about the proper way to conduct their ceremonies. But they would not have him as a convert. Eventually, when he died he was given an Islamic state funeral by the Shah. I find it rather ironic.'

'Yes,' said Miss Cama, 'it is sad. We began to refuse converts as a matter of precaution, so as not to antagonize the Muslims or Hindus amongst whom we have been living. Then it became a habit, then a matter of principle. And so it probably will remain until Sushyans comes and saves the whole world, the Zoroastrians and non-Zoroastrians.'

'Do you know?' I exclaimed, 'my ancestors had left Ireland for Canada in 1849 in very similar circumstances and for almost the same reasons yours had left Iran for India a thousand years ago? Poverty and religious harassment. Not active persecution, no. Roman Catholicism was legal in the United Kingdom by then, we even had the vote, but the poor Irish peasants were Catholics, while the landlords who exploited us were Protestants, mostly of English origin. And of course the British Government staunchly supported the Protestant landlords, especially during the Great Famine. Well, it was not quite so simple, but this is how we Irish-Canadians have been perceiving our past.'

I thought I saw a faint smile hovering around Miss Cama's lips. I knew that one quick way of making friends with Indians was to remind them that we Irish had also been victims of British imperialism.

'Have you read Thomas Moore's *Lalla Rookh*?' she asked me.

'Of course! It was one of the books that drove me into Orientalism.'

'Do you remember the story "The Fire Worshippers"? Of course you know we do not actually worship fire, we just regard it as the visible symbol of God. But anyway, the story is about a Persian Zoroastrian uprising against the Arabs. But Moore was really writing about an Irish uprising against the British, some time towards the end of the 18th century, I don't remember the exact date.'

'1798.'

'The name of the country gives the clue: It is the first time in English literature that Iran is called Iran instead of Persia. Iran is Erin.'

'I have often capitalized on the similarity of the name, suggesting a common Aryan origin, to impress my Iranian friends,' I said, 'but I didn't realize Moore was the first author to use the form Iran in English.'

'I am afraid I do not know any Persian, except for the Persian words in Urdu and Gujarati,' added Miss Cama regretfully. 'I can recite some prayers in Zend.'

'I don't know any Gaelic either,' I answered. 'My family considers itself Irish because of our Irish surname, O'Malley. But there is French and Scottish and Cree in us.'

'What is Cree?' Miss Cama seemed puzzled.

'Oh, you don't know? It is the largest Indian (I mean Canadian Indian, not India Indian) ethnic group in Canada, spread all the way from Northern Quebec to Alberta. My great-grandmother was a Cree from Manitoba. But I am as ignorant of Cree as I am of Irish. But if you're interested, I shall be pleased to teach you Persian if you would teach me Gujarati.'

'What do you want to learn Gujarati for?' asked Miss Cama.

I could detect a very, very slight trace of suspicion in her voice. After two or more centuries of Western colonialism Orientals have become suspicious of Westerners who want to learn their language. It is something instinctive, subconscious. They may not even be consciously aware of it. Some French-Canadians display a similar suspicion towards any outsiders who address them in French.

'There have been many works written about ancient Iran by Parsee scholars, most of them in English, but some in Gujarati,' I answered. It was true that I greatly admired (and still do) the works of Dhalla, Coyajee and other Parsee Iranologists, but I was not prepared to take the trouble to learn Gujarati just for that reason, especially since most of them had been writing in English. But I wanted to establish some lasting contact with the Parsee girl, since I did not intend to take advantage of the Curtises' hospitality for long. So, after all, Miss Cama was right if she suspected an ulterior motive in my interest in her language, but, in all honesty I can swear my motive was not an evil one.

By this time I had finished my supper. Miss Cama took away my dish and empty beer glass. She reappeared a few minutes later carrying a Chinese-looking teapot and a cup on a metal tray.

'Please!' I exclaimed. 'You did not eat supper with me because you said you had eaten earlier, but surely you could drink a cup of tea with me!'

Miss Cama smiled and brought another cup to the table. I was pleased. In Iran, and in England too, drinking a cup of tea together is a symbolic gesture of friendliness, if not of friendship. I could smell the fragrance of spices coming from the tea.

'Spicy tea! Reminds me of Zabul,' I exclaimed.

'Where is Zabul? in Iran?' asked Miss Cama.

'Yes,' I answered. 'Near the border of Afghanistan. Near Pakistan too. Capital of the District of Seistan. You may have noticed it on the map: a triangle of Iranian territory that cuts into Afghanistan. The people there have been somewhat influenced by Indian culture, at least superficially. They use a few Hindi words in their dialect, like *dobi* ('a washerwoman'), *natak* ('a dancer'); they use curry in their cooking and they drink tea with cinnamon and cardamom, although without milk.'

'Seistan! Of course I know Seistan! The home of Rustam!' exclaimed Miss Cama.

> 'And thou hast trod the sands of Seistan
> And seen the river of Helmand
> And the lake of Zirra.

What were you doing in Seistan? just travelling?'

'I stayed there almost six months until I was ousted by His Imperial Majesty's Police. I was studying the local dialect for my thesis.'

'Baluchi?'

'No, it is a Persian dialect, although Baluchi is spoken immediately to the South of Seistan, and there are many Baluchis living in Zabul. No one had ever studied or written anything about Seistani Persian before me.'

'That is exciting! But it reminds me: I must work on my thesis. You will excuse me.'

She led me into Jack's study and showed me the hundreds of books lining the walls.

'I am sure you will find something interesting here.'

She also pointed to a small table on which stood a decanter containing a dark liquid and several glasses.

'This is brandy, which Jack likes to offer his visitors. Please feel free to help yourself. He himself prefers whisky. Do you prefer whisky? I am sorry, I don't know where he keeps it. Now excuse me. Good night!'

She dashed upstairs. I have always been amazed at the ease with which Indian women move about in their saris. I heard her turning the key in her door. My immediate reaction was one of anger. What does she think? That I am going to abuse her hospitality and invade the privacy of her bedroom? I am an Oxford man! The primary aim of an Oxford education is to turn young men into gentlemen. Academic learning is of secondary importance. Or so we all claim. But then I thought: I shouldn't be silly. What does she know about me? Only what her landlord had told her, and he had not seen me since we graduated together. After that, with him in India, myself in Iran, then, with him back in England, myself back in Canada, we seldom wrote to each other. His demand from her to take care of his old friend, while he and his wife were stuck in Paris, must have come as a most annoying imposition upon her. I should be grateful that she did not show any sign of annoyance and comported herself as a most gracious hostess. Anyway, her locking the door did not necessarily indicate an apprehension of any misbehaviour on my part. Having to spend a night in that house alone with a man, however gentlemanly his behaviour, was a most embarrassing, indeed compromising situation for an Oriental girl. I am supposed to be an Orientalist. I should have understood it at once. She had to put up appearances, for herself if not for anyone else. Her refusal to have her dinner together with me had likewise been part of the attempt to keep her distance from a stranger.

A few minutes later I heard the sound of a typewriter

coming from upstairs, an indication that she had been telling me the truth about having to work on her thesis. I poured myself a glass of brandy, took a few sips, then put the glass down on the table and walked towards the bookshelves. As I should have expected, most of the books had to do with India. There were many Sanskrit and Hindi works in Devanagari script. I had learnt the Devanagari syllabary when I first came to Oxford as a 19-year-old Rhodes scholar, and joined, together with Jack Curtis, Professor Burrow's elementary Sanskrit class. But, almost without Greek and with very little Latin I was not well prepared for the study of dead languages. So, after one term I switched to Persian, a much, much easier, and, what is more important, a living language. Now I could just decipher the Devanagari titles. Most of the books however were in English, works about Indian history, Hindu religion, Indian ethnography, archaeology, you name it. There was a collection of grammars of most, if not all, languages of India. With some excitement I found among them St Clair Tisdall's *Simplified Grammar of the Gujarati Language* published in 1892. The Gujarati letters are similar to Devanagari, but lack the connecting line across the top and are written separately. Maybe Miss Cama would teach me her language from this book in exchange for Persian, I thought hopefully.

But I was feeling too agitated for serious study of Gujarati or anything else just then. Had to find something lighter to read. Somewhat incongruous among those scholarly works I found a volume of Kipling's poems. Incongruous? Not really. After all most of Kipling's writings had been about India. I took the book and sat with it at the table where my glass of brandy was waiting for me. Turning the pages at random I came across *The Ballad of East and West*:

'Oh, East is East, and West is West,
and never the twain shall meet,
Till Earth and sky stand presently
At God's great Judgment Seat;
But there is neither East nor West,
Border, nor Breed, nor Birth,
When two strong men stand face to face
Though they come from the ends of the earth!'

Of course Kipling was an imperialist. I don't like imperialism, British imperialism least of all with my Irish background. He had been called a racist. If so, he was prepared to make an exception. There were situations when race did not matter. I began to tinker with the second stanza:

'But there is neither East nor West,
Border, nor Breed, nor Birth,
When a strong man and a strong woman stand face to face,
Though they come from the ends of the earth!'

Kipling would not have approved. Not only because I had ruined the metre by inserting four extra syllables, but because I was challenging his fiercely masculine philosophy. Nevertheless I liked my paraphrase. I poured myself a second glass of brandy. My agitation was replaced by a feeling of fatigue. I replaced the book on the shelf and made my way upstairs to my bedroom. I could hear the sound of the typewriter coming from behind Miss Cama's door.

CHAPTER II

Jack Curtis and his wife Joyce arrived the following afternoon. The transport workers' strike in France had ended and they managed to get a plane. Jack had been my best friend in Oxford. We had matriculated at the same time and joined Professor Burrow's elementary Sanskrit class. With his public school Greek and Latin he was much better at it than I, and after one term I switched to Persian. Nevertheless our friendship was made, and we saw each other very often. Since I was at Exeter, he at Jesus, we couldn't help bumping into each other on the Turl. And of course we saw each other in the Indian Institute Library, although we couldn't talk there except in whispers. Before the founding of the new Oriental Institute the Indian Institute served as the centre of all Oriental studies in Oxford, not only Indian. The early British Orientalists had become interested in Persian, not so much because it was the language of Iran, but because it had been the language of administration and culture of the Mughal Empire. And this is how Persian had first been introduced into Oxford, from an Indian perspective.

To me the Indian Institute was the most interesting place in Oxford. It contained a small museum of Oriental art where I could have stayed for hours if I didn't feel I should spend that time studying in the Library. On the staircase hung a large brass tablet with a Sanskrit poem engraved upon it. I was surprised when Professor Burrow told me that the poem, praising the friendship of the two related Aryan races, the

British and the Indians, was not an extract from the Ramayana or the Mahabharata, but had been composed by one of his predecessors, Sir Monier Monier-Williams, the founder of the Institute. I knew that many Oxford scholars had composed poems in Latin and ancient Greek, but Sanskrit! The Indian Institute no longer exists as a separate unit. The Library has been moved across Parks Road into the New Bodleian, the art collection has been dispersed throughout the Ashmolean. The building has been put to other, non-Orientalist uses. Only the tablet with Professor Monier-Williams's Sanskrit poem remains to remind us of its past.

Of course it was our enthusiasm for the Orient which had drawn Jack and me together. We did have our differences. With my Irish background I loathed the British Empire, while Jack maintained that the Empire was not as evil as most people claim, that many imperialists like Sir William Jones (who had first discovered the kinship between European and Indian languages) or Sir Richard Burton had a genuine admiration for Oriental culture and had contributed a lot to make it known and appreciated in the West. We had some heated arguments about it until he shut me up by asking me why I had accepted a Rhodes Scholarship, founded by that arch-imperialist, Cecil Rhodes. Well, Indian students had been accepting Rhodes Scholarships, and this did not make them pro-British politically!

But our friendship survived more than political disagreement. It survived falling in love with the same girl. How many friends had turned into bitter enemies over the love for a woman! But in this case our shared aspiration had only drawn us closer together because we knew that the Indian girl from Somerville College was an unattainable ideal for both of us. We were undergraduates, while Kamala Devi wore a B.Lit.

gown over her sari, so she must have been several years older than us. She used to drive round Oxford in a red sports car. Few students owned cars. It wasn't against the rules, but it was discouraged by the Proctors. Jack had told me that she was a Rajput princess, that her great grandfather had hunted tigers and played polo with the Prince of Wales, the future Edward VII, and that she herself was invited to garden parties at Buckingham Palace and had been presented to the Queen. Princess or not, we were just boys to her and she was not in the least interested in us. In such a hopeless situation we couldn't possibly be rivals for her favour, and so our shared admiration for her drew us together instead of driving us apart. Soon enough we wisely forgot her.

One small incident had clouded our friendship, albeit for a very short time, during our second year in Oxford. We both rowed in the Eights. Jack was Stroke of the Jesus boat (he was left-handed) while I was Bow in the Exeter Eight. The Jesus boat was one place ahead of us. And our boat bumped theirs. Our College celebrated with a riotous bump supper, with champagne (not the most expensive kind of course) replacing the usual beer. I felt great! I was one of the nine (we must include the cox) heroes. But the following day, while recovering from the hangover, when I saw Jack in the Turl, there was a strangely hostile look in his eyes. 'You got me this time. You won't get me again!' he said gloomily. It may have been hangover also, for everyone, losers as well winners, gets drunk at the end of Eights Week after the long weeks of 'full training' when we were pledged not to touch alcohol, not even beer. Still, it wasn't the way a British sportsman accepts defeat. Within a few days we forgot about it, at least I did.

When we received our degrees, Jack in Sanskrit, me in Persian, he went to India, I to Iran. We corresponded between

Iran and India, we even planned to meet somewhere halfway, perhaps in Afghanistan, but when he returned to Oxford, where, having obtained his D.Phil. he was offered a lecturership in Sanskrit, and I returned to Canada, the correspondence almost stopped. He wrote to me saying that he was marrying a Miss Joyce Savage, an undergraduate at Lady Margaret Hall, without giving me any more information about her. But when I wrote to him that I was coming to Oxford for a sabbatical he very warmly invited me to stay with him before I could find permanent lodgings. He did not mention his tenant, Miss Cama.

Now we stood facing each other and recognized each other immediately. We had not changed much (I think we both got the same impression) except that we had both grown beards. Glad as I was to see him after so many years I was even more excited when I was introduced to his wife. This is strange. Until then I didn't care much to know what sort of woman he had married. One of those plain English girls, I thought. I didn't find English girls very attractive during my undergraduate days in Oxford. It had to do with my obsession with the Orient (and with Oriental girls). But this woman stunned me with the strength of her personality. She stood before me, a slender figure in a leather jacket, blue jeans and white sneakers, reddish-gold hair escaping from under a baseball cap. Her violet-blue eyes looked straight into mine without a trace of shyness. Her handshake was firm like a man's. I felt my own hand trembling, but maybe I was imagining. I hope I was imagining! Her moist crimson lips parted into a frank smile:

'I am so glad to meet you, Sean! Jack had told me so much about you!'

'All right, Joyce!' exclaimed Jack in a loud voice. 'Let's all of us have a drink and you can learn all about Sean directly from him. And I myself want to know what he has been doing during all these years.'

'All right, Jack,' answered Joyce. 'You start with your drinks, the three of you. I shall join you in a few minutes, but I am going to change first. I don't like sitting in my travelling clothes.'

Soon we were sitting, the four of us, each with a glass in our hand. Miss Cama refused whisky, but accepted a glass of sherry. But she was no longer Miss Cama to me. It seemed silly to call Jack Jack and to call his wife Mrs Curtis, especially since she had called me Sean as soon as we were introduced. It seemed equally silly to call Mrs Curtis, whom I had just met, Joyce and to call her friend, whom I had met the previous evening, Miss Cama. So Miss Cama became Morvarid. She didn't reciprocate immediately, a little overawed by my title of Professor, until I explained to her that in Canada every university teacher above the rank of lecturer is called a professor, that I was only an assistant professor, roughly corresponding to a British 'senior lecturer'.

'I would have been promoted to associate professor by now, if I had been more deferential towards the Dean and some other big shots at McGill,' I said grimly.

Meanwhile Joyce had changed from her leather jacket, jeans and sneakers into a tight-fitting black blouse, black corduroy trousers and high heels. I loved the apparent contrast of trousers and high heels. So provocatively feminine! The severe blackness of her costume was likewise relieved by a string of multi-coloured beads round her neck. Her lips and fingernails were painted a deep blood red. A pair of large earrings hung from her ears. Now that I could observe her better I could see some dark shadows lurking in her golden hair. I suspected that it was dyed. Why do dark-haired women so often dye their hair blonde? A girl with natural blonde hair may look sweet and innocent, but there is something provocatively sexy about hair dyed blonde. It excites and upsets me at the same time. It may look very attractive (it was very attractive in Joyce's case) but I feel it is a morbid attraction. It disturbs me. Also disturbing, although without a feeling of morbidity, I found the beauty of her figure, revealed by her costume: the firm breasts protruding under the tight blouse, the narrow waist, the slim legs within the narrow trousers. I felt that her apparently delicate limbs concealed a great physical strength and agility. Indeed, she told me she loved sports: tennis, swimming, rowing, most of all horse riding. As I watched her I felt the burning heat of desire harden and rise within me. Well, wasn't it natural for a man in his thirties to be attracted by a young woman in her twenties? Sure, it was most natural, but the woman was married. Married to my friend, at one time my best friend, too. I felt guilty. But that wasn't all. I felt I was being unfaithful to Morvarid. It was ridiculous. I had met Morvarid less than 24 hours before. What claim could she have upon my loyalty? And yet, and yet the feeling was there. I couldn't understand it.

I must however be fair to Joyce. I may be giving the impression that she was nothing but a sexy enchantress. She sure was that, but she was much more besides. I met in her an intellect equal to Morvarid's, which would explain why the two women had become close friends in spite of their very different personalities. Joyce had a BA in French literature and was writing a thesis about the influence of George Sand on the feminist movement. Likewise I suspected she was responsible for adding the modern abstract paintings to her husband's Oriental collection. Joyce knew a lot about the Orient, but, with the exception of India, about which she had learnt at first hand from her husband and from her friend Morvarid, it was all a literary Orient, as portrayed in French literature. She knew all about Camus's Algeria, about Pierre Loti's Turkey, about the Levant voyages of Chateaubriand and Lamartine. She had read the exotic poems of Leconte de Lisle. She even knew the French-Canadian Orientalist poet Paul Morin! About Iran she knew little although she had read Loti's travel diary, *Vers Ispahan*. She was a little disappointed when I told her that people no longer travelled from Shiraz to Isfahan by horse or camel, but by car, bus or plane. Still, I told her I did travel on horseback in Seistan, in the marshland villages of the Helmand delta where no car, not even a Jeep, could get through.

The discussion of French literature and my Iranian travels drew away my attention from Mrs Curtis's sexy appearance and I felt somewhat relieved. I could appreciate her as a person, not only as a woman. Nevertheless I felt I must start looking for lodgings as soon as possible, even before reapplying for permission to use the Bodleian Library. Of course I would see her and her husband often enough. I felt Jack and I had become estranged from one another and I was determined to reopen the communication. But most important was Morvarid. I must keep in touch with the Curtises for the sake of their tenant. But maybe I had enough in common with her to gain her interest, if not her friendship. She was a Parsee, a woman of Persian origin. Her people had long ago forgotten the Persian language, mingled with the Indians around them, but they have kept the ancient religion of Iran and the cultural heritage that went with it. I thought about the situation: I am an expert on Iran, the land of her ancestors; I speak the Persian language. She is writing a thesis about literary Orientalists who had admired Oriental women.

Would she accept the homage of an academic Orientalist? Our similar academic pursuits should provide a legitimate excuse to see each other often. But I must proceed carefully. She is an Oriental woman for all her English education. If I move too quickly from the intellectual plain to the romantic I may scare her off and lose her for ever, but if I am too shy I will get nowhere. To keep the right balance, that is the predicament. And the challenge!

CHAPTER III

I don't remember how long I had stayed with the Curtises. Maybe five days, maybe a week, maybe ten days. I never remember dates. I remember events, happy and painful, but what do I care about the date they had taken place? Joyce Curtis's physical looks no longer disturbed me. Not that I found her any less attractive, far from it, but I had got used to seeing her after the excitement of our first meeting. Like her heroine George Sand, she always wore trousers, except when going to lectures or other University functions requiring her to wear her academic gown. Among the many rules regulating the use of gowns was one prohibiting women members of the University, whether female dons with D.Phils. or first year undergraduates, from wearing trousers with academic dress. Actually the rule was instituted when I was in Oxford, and I remember an article in *Picture Post*, with several photographs of trousered girls, entitled 'Debag Oxford Women!'. In my time a girl wearing slacks was still a mysterious figure, perhaps a George Sand, a liberated woman proclaiming her defiance of convention; or a Joan of Arc, a mystic who had made a vow of chastity and was sending a warning to all men not to look upon her as a woman, her beauty even more alluring because forbidden. But by the time of my return to Oxford women had begun to wear trousers as normal everyday wear, not necessarily a statement of defiant feminism. Most girls looked very attractive in slacks, but the feeling of mystery was gone.

I found both women, Morvarid and Joyce, extremely

beautiful. I tried to analyse their beauty. To try to compare them was too hard. It was like trying to compare Windsor Castle with the Taj Mahal. Their styles are fundamentally different. So it is with the beauty of women. If we can't compare them, we can at least try to label them. We call the beauty of Windsor Castle Gothic, that of the Taj Mahal Indo-Islamic or Indo-Iranian. But women are more difficult to label. Oriental and Occidental? True as far is it goes, but very inadequate. Maybe I could label Morvarid's beauty as 'spiritual', Joyce's as 'sensual'. I remembered seeing in an arts magazine the copy of a painting of two women entitled 'Love Sacred and Profane'. It had been many many years ago (I was a teenager at the time). I don't remember the name of the painter. I don't even remember the style. Could have been Italian Renaissance, could have been British Pre-Raphaelite. All I remember is that the woman representing love sacred was seated, wrapped in a long robe, while her companion, representing love profane, was standing, naked except for her long hair. The two women in the painting didn't resemble Morvarid and Joyce at all, but the idea was right: love sacred and profane.

There was, or at least I saw something sacred about Morvarid. With her dark face, wrapped in her blue sari she reminded me of a Byzantine Madonna or of the three female figures in sari-like dresses in Andrei Rublov's painting supposed to represent the Holy Trinity. If Joyce's beauty excited, even disturbed me, Morvarid's mere presence brought upon me a feeling of tranquillity, of inner peace, something like the Nirvana of the Buddhists.

Was sacred or spiritual love superior to the sensual or 'profane'? Brought up a strict Catholic I had believed that 'pure' or spiritual love was the only kind permitted. It was OK to love a girl so long as that love was pure. True, physical love was also created by God, but that would take care of itself after marriage. Until then any sexual fantasy was a sin, to be driven away by prayer. An impossible requirement which had caused me much anguish. The storm of Vatican II had blown away the dark clouds of my guilt feelings. Did I then have to choose one or the other kind of love, or could I have both, and if so, how?

These questions threw my mind back a decade and a half earlier to my undergraduate days and the long fireside discussions we used to have in each other's college rooms, usually on Saturday nights, over endless bottles of beer. The discussion always began with sports, but the conversational possibilities of this subject are limited, and even young Englishmen can't keep it up for longer than ten minutes. Well, fifteen minutes. After that introduction we discussed almost everything: art, literature, philosophy, religion. Politics? Never! Only Poles and Indians had the ill manners to argue which imperialism was worse: Russian or British? Then, around midnight would come the subject foremost in everyone's mind: girls. (The subject of girls would come earlier if there was sherry or whisky as an alternative to beer.) The ratio of men and women in the University was about six to one, and this created a tension probably unknown to our predecessors before the first women's colleges, Lady Margaret Hall and Somerville were founded in 1878. Some pretended to postpone any serious interest in girls until they get their degrees and 'go down' into the world. Only after much drink did they confess their anxiety. (Some may have belonged to a secret order, having as its patron a certain Oscar Wilde from Magdalen, whose members had to renounce any romantic interest in girls. They had other interests, which were illegal in Britain at the time, hence the necessity for the strictest secrecy.)

Thus, when contemplating the very different beauty of Morvarid and Joyce I remembered the words of Percy Proudfoot that a man, especially an artist or a poet (he himself was a poet, a great poet in his own estimation) needs the love of two women, either two wives, or, should that cause legal problems, a wife and a mistress, or two mistresses, one for sensual love, the other as a romantic ideal. He had a BA in Classics or 'Greats' and spoke with authority to us, mere undergraduates.

'But how many women will accept such a situation?' someone asked. 'Won't they be jealous of each other?'

'Why should they?' retorted the great man with a big puff of smoke from his pipe. 'Their spheres are different. Your doctor and your clergyman aren't jealous of each other. One looks after the well-being of your body, the other after your soul.'

For various reasons, few of us were convinced. Myself, although I found the proposition logical, could not accept it on moral grounds. I felt it would have been unfair to the two women concerned. Probably my Catholic background had to do with it. Several participants in the debate staunchly maintained that romantic love was a myth invented by neurotic poets without any basis in reality. Sexual attraction was the only thing there was to love. Quoting (or misquoting) Dr Freud they maintained that romantic love was nothing but a sublimation of that sexual urge. The sooner we realize it the better. Charles Young who was reading German literature argued that the same woman could satisfy our sexual and our romantic longing. Indeed, when we dream of two or more different women they are merely two aspects of the same woman whom we are bound to find if we persist in seeking her. She is our soul or 'anima'. I felt myself in agreement with Charles. Moreover I felt absolutely certain that I would have to seek my anima in the Orient. After several painful experiences with Oriental girls in Oxford and in Iran I returned to Canada, determined to forget the Orient. My thesis, and then my job, would not allow it. I went with Canadian girls, high-spirited girls in blue jeans. They were attractive girls. Some of them were beautiful girls. Yet, however much I may have got involved with any of them, I always felt there was something missing, I couldn't quite define what. Each affair had ended with a bitter taste in my mouth. And now the Orient had come back to me in the person of Morvarid.

Back to the present: There was something in my hosts' household which I did not like. I felt the Curtises were exploiting Morvarid. She did all the cooking and much of the housework. This on top of her studies. Sure, I enjoyed her cooking. Both Jack and Joyce loved hot curry, and when Morvarid learned that I did too, she made it much hotter than the dinner she had served me upon my arrival. But, my God, she was supposed to be their tenant, not their servant! Presumably she was paying rent. I felt really angry: who do the Curtises think they are, having the audacity to exploit an Indian student girl? Damn British imperialists! But I'd better shut up. I was their guest after all. Well, I'd better find myself lodgings soon and get out of that house. I must admit I felt a little angry with Morvarid also for allowing them to exploit her. I must speak to her and tell her to stand up and refuse to take it any longer. But not now while I am her landlords' guest. I must move out soon. It will give me more freedom to speak to her and in this way bring me nearer to her in the long run.

CHAPTER IV

I am walking the streets of Oxford looking for lodgings. I began in North Oxford in order to be within the neighbourhood of Morvarid. North Oxford is the residential area where most of the married dons live. Victorian brick houses in flowery gardens, not very different looking from middle class suburbs around other English cities. Four out of the five women's colleges are situated in that area. But then it occurred to me that, unless I live in the immediate neighbourhood, on the same street, as the girl I aspire towards, I am not very likely to run into her. I had become aware of that during my undergraduate days. I'd better settle downtown to be near the libraries. I shall have a better chance of meeting Morvarid in one of the Bodleian's reading rooms or in Broad Street than in the tree-shaded avenues of North Oxford.

I walk the streets of downtown Oxford among the Colleges. The Gothic architecture which I love. Real Gothic and Victorian Gothic. I don't mind Victorian Gothic. The Romantics and the Victorians felt a nostalgia for the middle ages. We, the latter-day romantics feel a nostalgia for the 19th century, a time before the streets of Oxford were filled with noisy motor-cars. Not much space for trees in the narrow streets. But I see the tops of many trees above the long high walls surrounding the college gardens. The garden walls of Oxford, the garden walls of Iran!

It is strange that Oxford, for several centuries a centre of Oriental learning, does not present any examples of Oriental architecture. Not even bad Oriental architecture like the Prince Regent's Brighton. Even the Indian Institute, which I had found so fascinating as an undergraduate, is built in a cold neo-classical style, lacking the warmth of the Gothic or the baroque. But the long, high, mysterious walls surrounding the college gardens, these are, unintentionally I am sure, the most Oriental features of Oxford landscape. In Iran you see them everywhere, even in the modern capital of Tehran, the walls surrounding the British and Russian Embassies. In the provincial towns those walls are universal. Sometimes in the evening, when walking the streets of Zabul I could hear coming over a garden wall a lively conversation of women's voices and laughter. Sometimes a song, sung either in literary Persian or in the Seistani dialect (occasionally in Baluchi), accompanied by the strings of the *santoor*, the Iranian dulcimer. A women's tea party, absolutely forbidden to any male, Muslim or infidel!

There were girls in the streets of Oxford. I found I liked English girls now better than I did during my undergraduate days. Was it because most of them were wearing slacks or jeans as the new fashion dictated? Or was it because of my recently awakened nostalgia for Oxford? I appreciated their looks, but my heart was not with them.

I felt like a ghost haunting Oxford. The place looked familiar, but, except for Jack Curtis, I knew no one. My tutors were dead or retired, living in Brighton or Bournemouth or I don't know where. My fellow students had jobs all over Britain if not all over the world. Why did I choose to write a history of Persian studies in Oxford as my sabbatical project? True, I was a persona non grata in Iran, but there are thousands of unedited, almost unknown, Persian manuscripts in the libraries of India, Pakistan and Turkey. But if I had gone elsewhere I wouldn't have met Morvarid. I don't know. Perhaps I would have met her somewhere else. One thing I had learnt from the Iranians was their fatalism. Makes life easier. Something had drawn me back to Oxford. I think I have come to understand the psychological basis of our belief in ghosts. If, after we die, we can freely travel all over the universe with the speed of thought, faster than the speed of light, surely we will want to revisit the places we had loved during our life on earth. Naturally we expect the same from those who have gone before us. Oxford is supposed to be haunted by more ghosts than any other city in England: John Ruskin, William Morris, Matthew Arnold, Lewis Carroll and many, many others. I myself have never seen a ghost, but several Exeter undergraduates had solemnly declared they had seen the ghost of William Morris lurking in the dark passage from Exeter's First Quadrangle to the Fellows' Garden. True, they admitted they were drunk at the time, but never-theless . . . So, maybe I shall also return to Oxford after I die. Maybe Morvarid will accept to come with me. Holding hands we shall effortlessly glide through walls and closed doors or float over the roof-tops. And there may be talk in the common rooms about a strange man with a beard and a woman wrapped in a sari haunting the former Indian Institute.

Back to reality, man! There aren't many rooming-houses in the central college area. But why don't I try Ship Street? There is a house there with a large first floor window covered by an elaborate wrought-iron grille in the Spanish style, just a few steps from the main entrance to Exeter across the Turl, and about five minutes' walk from the Bodleian Library. I was told by the landlady that all her rooms, including the room with the Spanish window, were occupied. I had to move further. I walked down the Cornmarket and continued on St Aldate's.

Just before reaching the Tom Tower I turned right into Pembroke Street. At no. * I was shown a fairly large room with a window overlooking St Aldate's Church and Pembroke College.

'Can you hear Great Tom here?' I asked the landlady.

'Oh yes, Sir!' she answered eagerly. 'It rings one hundred and one times every evening, 5 minutes after 9. It don't bother me. And I don't think it bothers any of the gentlemen lodging here.'

I decided to take that room. But that was after my long talk with Jack.

CHAPTER V

The evening before I found the room on Pembroke Street I had returned to the Curtises' home as usual. Jack opened the door for me.

'The girls have gone to a dinner and some kind of meeting in LMH' he announced. 'Have you eaten?' I had eaten in town. 'Good! We men can have a talk at last. We haven't really had a talk since you arrived, a private talk I mean. Brandy or whisky? Whisky? Good! I prefer whisky.'

We settled in his study with a bottle of whisky and a bucket of ice cubes. I noticed he was drinking fast.

'You like Morvarid, don't you?' he shot suddenly. I thought I could detect a tone of challenge in his voice.

'A charming girl!' I answered. 'Intelligent too.'

'Only intelligent?' he exclaimed. 'She is absolutely brilliant! She says she wants to go back to India when she gets her D.Phil. But she has a great future in front of her, right here, in Oxford! Elizabeth Jameson tells me . . . '

'Who is Elizabeth Jameson?'

'She is the Gertrude Bell Professor of English Lit at LMH. She wants Morvarid to stay on as a tutor and eventually to succeed her as the Bell Professor of English.'

I couldn't resist the temptation to tease him: 'Will you accept an Indian woman in a sari to be a professor of your own English literature at your most prestigious University?'

Jack's face put on a pompous look: 'We have no racial discrimination in this University. We take the best qualified, whatever their national origin. Remember Professor Radhakrishnan and his turban?'

'No. He was before my time.'

'Anyway, Morvarid is by far better qualified than any Englishwoman.'

I remembered that until some decades ago Trinity College (the one in Oxford, not the one in Dublin) was refusing to admit non-white undergraduates, but the past is the past. Nowadays, I think that however much racism may be lingering on among the less educated English lower and middle classes, it has no place in Oxford or other British universities. I myself, like most Canadians, tend to be rather smug about our vaunted lack of racism in Canada. It hasn't always been so. I remembered some horror stories told by my half-Cree grandmother. But that had been long ago!

'I agree with you,' I answered in a conciliatory tone. 'Morvarid is a wonderful woman, in more ways than one.'

Jack took another gulp of whisky.

'Are you really interested in her? I mean, seriously?' he asked me.

'Well, yes,' I answered. Now it was my turn to take a large sip of whisky. 'I think I am beginning to fall in love with her.'

It was an understatement. By that time I did not think, I was damn sure I was in love with Morvarid, not just beginning to.

'Well, I think you'd better stop before you get more seriously involved,' said Jack grimly. 'You know the Zoroastrians don't intermarry with other religions. And you can't become a Zoroastrian either, because they won't take you, you know that. And if you are thinking of having an affair with her without marriage, you know the East. I don't think Iran is very different from India in this respect. Better leave her alone.'

34

I banged the glass against the table, spilling half of its contents. Fortunately the glass did not break.

'Who the Hell are you taking me for?' I shouted. 'I may be tempted to have an affair with some other woman, but not with Morvarid! I respect Morvarid. She is the most honourable girl I had ever met!'

'Forgive me,' answered Jack extending his hand. 'I have never doubted you are an honourable man. I know you would never act dishonourably towards Morvarid; or towards any woman for that matter. You are an Oxford man. You could almost be an Englishman,' he added without a trace of irony in his voice. I knew it was the highest compliment he could pay me.

'But are you sure it is her you love?' he continued. 'I mean, do you love her as a woman, not just as a symbol of a culture which you find attractive?'

'Culture is important in a girl,' I answered. 'At least it is important to me. I wouldn't like to marry a girl without a culture and a tradition behind her. I had met some East Indian girls from Trinidad and Guiana. Very beautiful girls. Very nice girls. But they had no culture. No, I am being unfair to them. I mean, whatever culture they had, it was cosmopolitan West Indian or Anglo-Canadian. They spoke nothing but English, which is all right with me, but they didn't even know what language their ancestors had spoken in India or which province of India they had originally come from. They knew they were Hindu or Muslim, but that meant little to them in our secularized Western world. I need a woman with a tradition behind her.'

'And do you think this particular woman, with the tradition you appreciate, will marry you, against that tradition?'

'I don't know,' I answered. 'I don't think I should make such a proposal to her at this stage. Probably would scare her off. Just now I enjoy her conversation. I enjoy her presence. That will do for the moment.'

'Although you seem to be in such a hurry to find lodgings, my house will always be open to you whenever you want to see her,' answered Jack. 'Because, if you are thinking of taking her out to dinners and places you will find her rather reluctant. But where will it get you? You will enjoy her conversation, you will get even more involved with her than you are now, you will ask her to marry you, she will say no. What then? Isn't it better to stop now, while you can, to spare yourself the suffering in the future?'

'It is a risk all of us lovers have to take,' I answered. 'At least I shall have the satisfaction of having done my utmost to win her. But if I back out I will never be able to forgive myself. Of course I have no right to demand of her that she should betray the laws of her religion for me. It will be for her to decide.'

I remembered going for a tour of Iran in a hired Tehran taxi with three other foreign students. The leader of our little expedition, Gian Roberto was studying all the different religions of Iran and was going to introduce us to some Zoroastrians in Kerman. Perhaps, I thought, I would meet some interesting girls there, more friendly than Muslim girls. 'Can *Zartoshtis* marry people of other religions?' I asked our expert guide. '*Agar 'ashegh mishand* (If they fall in love),' answered the Italian student in Persian. (We always spoke Persian to each other, except when we didn't want to be understood by the locals.)

'I wish you luck,' answered Jack with a tone of sarcasm in his voice. 'But, to tell you frankly, I don't think Morvarid will ever get married, to you or to anyone else. She is too scholarly for that, too immersed in her studies to think of men and marriage.'

'Come on, Jack!' I exclaimed in surprise. 'A glamorous girl like her!'

'You find her glamorous in her saris,' answered Jack coolly, 'but you are getting the wrong message. You know Iran, but you don't know India or Indian women. Out of ten Indian girls who wear the sari in the West only one does so with the conscious intention to look glamorous, to impress men, Indian men or Western men. The other nine wear saris because it is the proper thing to wear, it is traditional, it is modest. They don't want to show their legs. They may have a Western university education, they may know English better than their own language, but their attachment to their religion, to their tradition is something deep, deep inside them. And Morvarid is one of those nine.'

I felt Jack was trying to discourage me from my aspirations towards Morvarid. But why? Out of jealousy? But he was married, presumably happily. Did he think I wasn't good enough for Morvarid? What business of his was that? Did he feel responsible to protect her in his capacity as her landlord? In my time Oxford landlords did have some responsibility to look after the morality of their undergraduate tenants, namely to ensure that no visitors of the opposite sex were present in their rooms after 10 p.m. I remember my landlady bursting into my room every evening: 'Sorry to disturb you, Mr O'Malley. I must ensure all ladies are out, Mr O'Malley.' (glancing under my bed). 'Otherwise I shall lose my licence, Mr O'Malley.' But this was as far as the powers of the landlords went, and they applied only to undergraduates. Morvarid was a D.Phil. student.

'I have known Morvarid much longer than you,' continued

Jack. The authority of this statement could not be challenged. He had known her for at least a couple of years, while I knew her for maybe ten days. 'I am speaking from personal experience.' He paused and took a long drought of whisky. 'You see, I had myself asked her to marry me at one time.'

For a moment I couldn't talk, overtaken by surprise. At last I said:

'I assume it must have been before you met Joyce. Morvarid refused you, probably for religious reasons, so you married another girl.'

'She didn't give me a categorical refusal,' answered Jack with a note of sadness in his voice. 'She merely said she thought I would be happier if I married a girl of my own nationality and religion.' (Jack was a rather indifferent member of the Church of England.) 'She even said she knew a girl who was just right for me, her best friend, Joyce Savage. She said she had wanted me to meet her before, but somehow never got down to introducing us. Now she insisted I must meet her friend. I told her I wasn't interested in her Joyce or in any other woman, but in her. She told me that if I refused to meet her friend she herself would stop seeing me and that would be the end of our friendship.'

'Was she your tenant at the time?' I interjected.

'Of course not!' he answered, as if surprised at my question. 'But we used to meet fairly often. We sat for many hours in cafes. Sometimes she invited me for tea in her room in LMH, sometimes, not often, she accepted my invitation for dinner. I had no choice but to agree to her strange demand: "All right, I shall meet your friend. I promise to . . . to be polite to her. And will you marry me afterwards?" "I cannot promise you anything" she answered. "I hope you will like her. I am sure she will like you." "And suppose I don't like her?" I retorted (I was beginning to hate her, I mean Joyce, not Morvarid). "Will you marry me then?" "I told you I cannot promise anything, but I shall think about it, if you do meet my friend and still prefer me." "But are you sure she will like me?" I asked in desperation. "Suppose she doesn't?" "I shall consider your proposal if it still stands after you have met Joyce," she answered, "but I am telling you for the third time I cannot promise." '

'So,' continued Jack, 'she invited me for tea another time. Unlike the previous occasions, this time I went most reluctantly. I was going to be introduced to her friend Joyce. Joyce was not there when I arrived. "Would you like a cup of tea while we are waiting or shall we wait for Joyce?" asked Morvarid. "She should be here soon." She poured me a cup of tea, but I couldn't touch it. I wanted that Joyce to come and have it over with her! Morvarid tried to start a casual conversation, but I wasn't in a talking mood. After what seemed to me half an hour, but what probably was no more than a few minutes, there was a knock at the door and I saw Joyce for the first time.'

Jack took another gulp of whisky: 'I was stunned! I had expected to see another plain English undergraduate girl, there are so many of them in Oxford, but Joyce was . . . , well, I don't have to describe her to you. You have met her.'

'Yes, Joyce is a most charming woman,' I answered. I suppose this was the polite thing to say to a man about his wife. 'Of course she is charming in a very different way from Morvarid,' I added.

'Exactly so!' exclaimed Jack, swallowing more whisky. 'As I watched the two of them, the Indian woman wrapped in her sari, beautiful, but unapproachable, like a painting of the goddess Saraswati, and the English girl at ease in blue jeans, I found them like the antitheses of each other. I think I was still in love with Morvarid, but . . . I don't know: Had I ever loved her as a woman or only as a symbol of the Orient? But I felt all the excitement of meeting Joyce. I felt completely at ease with her, as if I had known her for months. She spoke of her love of horse-riding. Then Morvarid suggested: "You are so fond of horse-riding, both of you. Why don't you go for a ride together one of these days?"'

I could guess what was coming. All of us, well, most of us find it very romantic to go on a horse promenade with a pretty girl, but it is the English romantics who have elevated horse-riding to an erotic symbol. Among the upper class English you invite a girl for a horse ride as you would invite her to a movie or a dinner or a dance. I remember seeing a cartoon (I think it was in one of André Maurois's amusing handbooks about England) depicting a Frenchman and an Englishman meeting a beautiful girl in the street. Above the heads of the two men are shown the fantasies she provokes in them: the Frenchman imagines her stark naked, but the Englishman pictures her in a riding costume with tight-fitting jodhpurs. I had read in a British tabloid newspaper (I forgot which) that Lord Mountbatten, the last Viceroy of India, used to collect photographs of women in riding breeches or jodhpurs, clipped from equestrian magazines. This eroticizing of horse-riding may have its origin in the not so distant past when that sport was providing one of the few occasions when fashionable ladies were permitted to show off the gracefulness of their figures by wearing trousers. So I wasn't surprised to hear that Jack and Joyce had eagerly taken up Morvarid's suggestion.

'There was a certain Mr Bradley who owned a riding school in Botley,' Jack was telling me. 'You could also hire horses from him. Very interesting man, Mr Bradley. Had been an officer in the Indian Army. Spoke Urdu, Punjabi, Nepali. Now he has retired, may be dead for all I know, and the riding school has closed down. Joyce and I hired a pair of horses from him. Joyce looked absolutely lovely in her riding outfit! So slender in her jodhpurs! We rode towards Boar's Hill. Ever been to Boar's Hill?'

'No,' I answered. 'I think I know Oxford pretty well, but the district around hardly at all.'

'There is a very fine view of the city from the Hill,' said Jack. 'We passed by a Gipsy camp. Motor trailers only. No more horse caravans. Remember their caravans rolling slowly along the High? I wondered whether Joyce had some Gipsy blood. That would have made her at least a little Oriental. Her hair is really quite dark. She hadn't dyed it blonde yet. At last we arrived on Boar's Hill. It was a hot sunny day and we found shelter from the sun in a small wooded area. We tied our horses to two trees and spread a blanket on the ground. Joyce had made a couple of sandwiches and I had packed a small bottle of French wine. As your poet Omar Khayyam says (By 'your poet' Jack no doubt meant that Khayyam belonged to Persian scholars like myself as well as to native Persians):

> "Here with a Loaf of Bread beneath the Bough,
> A Flask of Wine, a Book of Verse – and Thou
> Beside me singing in the Wilderness –
> And Wilderness is Paradise enow."

How does it go in the original? OK, never mind,' continued Jack. 'After we finished the sandwiches and the wine we sat for a while in silence. Then I put my arm round her shoulder, drew her towards me and kissed her on the cheek. She turned her face towards me and our lips met in a long, long kiss. We sank to the ground. I felt a fire burning within me. I could no longer control myself. With my heart pounding like Great Tom I undid the buckle of her belt and opened the zipper of her jodhpurs. She didn't protest. After that, well, you can guess, I don't need to tell you.' His voice trembled.

Yes, I could guess. But I was wondering: Why is he telling me all this? Of course he is drunk. An Englishman doesn't talk about the most intimate personal things unless he is really drunk. Tomorrow he will regret what he has told me. If he remembers. Hopefully he won't remember.

'The ecstasy that girl has given me!' he continued after another sip of whisky. 'And what did I get from Morvarid? Why, I had known her for almost a year, yet not once did I dare to kiss her cheek or to put my arm round her. I may have loved her, but she was taboo to me. Well, I was through with her. And with all Oriental women. I had an English girl!'

I began to suspect the reason for this talk. Drink helped of course, it loosened his inhibitions, but it wasn't the cause of it. He wasn't just talking to me. He was using me as a sounding-board, but he was really talking to himself. He was trying to convince himself that he had done the wise thing to give up Morvarid for Joyce. Obviously he loved his wife intensely. I could feel that from the passionate way he was talking about their first love-making. Very likely he had been going through the same experience every night. Then why did he feel the need to convince himself? I am not a psychologist, so I may have been mistaken, but I began to suspect that, for all his ardent love for Joyce, deep, deep in his subconscious he still loved Morvarid.

'I don't know how long we lay in each other's arms,' Jack resumed his narrative. 'Probably it wasn't more than a few minutes, but time had stopped for us. At least it had stopped for me. Slowly I got up. Joyce rose likewise and pulled up her jodhpurs. She fastened the zipper and buckled her belt. To my fantasy she seemed like Joan of Arc putting on her armour. She opened her handbag, took out a small mirror, put on fresh lipstick and began to comb her hair. 'Will you marry me, Joyce?' I asked her. It was the decent thing to say to her, wasn't it, after what we . . . after what I had done to her. But I was glad to say it! I really loved her and wanted to marry her. I really was hoping that she would accept. 'But aren't you almost engaged to Morvarid?' she asked me. 'No, I am not!' I almost shouted. 'It is true that I had asked her to marry me, but she didn't accept. Surely I have no obligations towards a girl who doesn't want me! I did love her once, at least I thought I did. Now I see I had loved her as a symbol of a country and a culture I admired, but not as a man loves a woman, not as I love you, Joyce.'

A moment of silence followed.

'I can see that Joyce has accepted your proposal' I said. 'You are married to her.'

'She said she would like to think about it. We rode back from Boar's Hill in silence. We rode slowly. You should never let your horse trot or canter downhill, you know. By the time we reached Mr Bradley's stables she gave me her answer. I was happy. The hard thing was to face Morvarid. No, it wasn't guilt. I had nothing to feel guilty about. She didn't want me. Actually I was going to do what she had recommended. It wasn't guilt; it was shame; it was my wounded pride; my reluctance to admit defeat. I had unequivocally assured her that I wasn't interested in Joyce or in any other woman except her, Morvarid, and if I was agreeing to meet Joyce it was only at her insistence. And now I was going to tell her that I was going to marry Joyce! I felt like a dog. "You were right" I told her, my eyes cast down, ashamed to look her in the face. "I feel Joyce is the right girl for me. But I hope we shall remain friends." "Yes, I know," Morvarid answered. "Joyce has told me you have asked her to marry you. I am very pleased for both of you. Of course we shall remain friends, even more than before, now that you are going to marry my best friend." I looked up. I thought I saw tears shining in her eyes, but I am not sure. There is an element of melancholy in every separation and now the separation between her and me had become final. We would remain friends, but . . . '

He fell silent and drank more whisky.

'I understand you very well,' I said. 'You had done nothing wrong. You had no obligations towards Morvarid, since she didn't accept your proposal. But it is always humiliating to admit defeat. But, with this experience between the two of you, don't you find it, what shall I say, embarrassing to have her living with you as your tenant?'

'It wasn't my idea,' answered Jack. 'It was Joyce's idea. She insisted Morvarid should move in with us when we bought this house. At that time Morvarid had to vacate her room in LMH. Even overseas students can't stay in college more than a couple of years. She had been allowed a room for an extra year because she was given an appointment as a temporary lecturer, replacing a woman tutor who had gone on sabbatical. But it was only a temporary appointment and she had to vacate the room at the end of the academic year. Of course, when she gets her D.Phil. and a permanent appointment as a tutor,' (Jack seemed perfectly confident that LMH would offer her the post) 'she will be entitled to a room in college. But I hope she will stay with us. You have asked me whether I have felt embarrassed. In the beginning, yes, somewhat. But not any longer. What is past is past. We are good friends. One day

Joyce and I will have children. I hope Morvarid will help us to bring them up . . . '

I felt furious. 'What cheek he has!' I thought. 'Not satisfied with having made her his cook he wants her to become an ayah for his little bastards!' But I held my peace.

'Meanwhile you'll be most welcome to visit us as often as you like. Morvarid will be pleased to see you too. But be careful not to get too . . . too . . . romantic with her.'

I thought I discerned a hint of threat, or at least of warning in his voice.

CHAPTER VI

My head was full of confusion with what I had heard. On the one hand I was pleased Morvarid had turned down Jack's proposal. His loss was my chance. But, judging from his experience she will most likely refuse me too, for the same reasons. Had she been a Muslim she would no doubt have demanded that Jack or I or any Western suitor should accept her religion. But I couldn't become a Zoroastrian even if I wanted to. How strongly was she attached to the Zoroastrian faith? '*Agar 'ashegh mishand* (If they fall in love)' I remembered Gian Roberto's words. Could I succeed where Jack had failed? I thought Jack was a fool. His love had lacked determination. He had allowed himself to be turned away from his true love by a sexy girl. Sure, Joyce was a very fine woman, beautiful (in a non-Oriental way), warm, intelligent, well educated (Oxford-educated), but somehow I couldn't help feeling Morvarid was superior to her. Maybe it was my Orientalist bias, racism in reverse.

In Joseph Conrad's novel *The Rescue* Captain Tom Lingard abandons the sweet, shy Indonesian princess, Immada for the sake of an arrogant English virago, Edith Travers with whom he has become infatuated. He loses his honour (Immada's brother, Hassim had saved his life). He doesn't even get Edith who is married to a stupid prig. He loses both women, Immada to her death, Edith to her husband. When I first read the novel as a teenager I felt a certain contempt for Lingard, not so much for his dishonourable behaviour, but because I thought he was a fool. I liked Immada better than Edith. There seems to be a pattern in literature of a white man abandoning a sweet and shy Oriental girl for a tough western virago. There is Lt Pinkerton in Puccini's opera *Madama Butterfly*, certainly a cad, but even worse: a fool.

I wondered whether racism had not played a part in Jack's decision to give up Morvarid for Joyce. 'I was through with her. And with all Oriental women. I had an English girl!' There is a kind of 'limited' racism, found even among educated British, which accepts friendship with people of all races and colours, but, nevertheless, regards interracial marriage as taboo. In Jack's case it would have been subconscious of course, an atavistic throwback.

They say one bird in the hand is better than two in the bush. A Polish friend of mine had told me the Polish version of this proverb: Better a sparrow in hand than a dove on the roof. But suppose the bird which has landed on our roof is not a humble dove but Simorgh or Hudhud or 'Anqa or the Phoenix? Wouldn't most of us climb the roof to catch her, however slim the chance? There had been during my undergraduate days an awesome sport being practised in Oxford, mercifully out of fashion nowadays, a game as deadly as Spanish bullfighting, but without the sunshine and without the cheering crowds, a game played anonymously in the darkness of the night. It was a sort of mountaineering, but, instead of natural mountains, the nocturnal 'alpinists', without proper equipment, used to climb the roofs of various University buildings, the towers and the spires: the Martyrs' Memorial (relatively easy), the dome of Radcliffe Camera, the Tom Tower, the spire of St Mary's. Of course the sport was strictly forbidden both by the Proctors and by Thames Valley Police. Hence it had to be pursued under the cover of darkness. The climbers were regarded as heroes by most undergraduates, crazy heroes no doubt, but heroes nevertheless. But theirs was an anonymous glory. The Proctors threatened expulsion from the University as punishment. So the victorious climber would leave a memento on top of a disturbed dreaming spire, a college scarf, or a stolen police helmet. Presumably a few close friends would be in the know and congratulate him by standing him drinks in the pub. Yet occasionally the foolhardy mountaineer would break out of anonymity and have his name printed in the *Oxford Mail*, but at the price of his life, when his shattered body would be found at the foot of a tower on a misty morning. I never knew the motivation which drove the night climbers. Was it simple bravado? Or did they, at least some of them, try to impress their girlfriends? Wouldn't I have climbed any spire in Oxford if Morvarid had asked me to? But of course she would never make such a demand of Jack or of me or of any other man. Indeed, she would have been horrified at the idea.

I have called Jack a fool, because he had thrown away a chance, however slim. If Morvarid had told him a categorical 'no' and perhaps refused to see him any more (some girls refuse to continue seeing a man whose proposal they reject), well, it is silly to go after a girl who refuses to have anything to do with you. Only boys in their teens or early twenties pine after a lost love. But all Morvarid had asked him to do was to meet her friend Joyce. If he didn't like Joyce she would have considered him. But the fool jumped for Joyce and quickly renounced his love for Morvarid. Did he really? I suspected that deep, deep inside him he still loved her. He had arranged himself very comfortably with two women: a sensual love with his wife and a platonic friendship with his tenant. And he wanted to keep it that way. His affirmation that Morvarid was 'too scholarly' to get married was probably wishful thinking.

Unlike Christians, Hindus or Buddhists the Zoroastrians do not believe in the supposed virtue of celibacy.

How did the two women take it? I thought I understood Joyce. A young don was a good catch. She wanted her husband and her friend with her, especially since she saw nothing in Jack's behaviour to make her jealous. Morvarid was more difficult to understand. Her personality was deeper, more complex. What was her motive in urging Jack to marry Joyce when he had proposed to her? Did she really mean it? Or did she want to test the determination of his love? I suspected the latter. She must have loved Jack. Otherwise why didn't she say a categorical 'no' to his proposal? Maybe she felt divided between her love for Jack and her fidelity to her faith and tradition? Maybe she wanted fate, as personified by Joyce, to decide for her? But why, later on, did she accept to become the tenant of a man who had once declared his love for her and for whom apparently she had also felt some affection? No doubt she thought it was all over for both of them, with him happily married to her friend. It was nice to stay with a pair of friends, better than with a strange landlord or landlady. Silly innocent girl! Silly in spite of all her bookish learning. She did not see through Jack. I have often been told a woman can see through another woman the way a man cannot. The opposite also is true. A man can see through another man the way a woman can't. I could see that Jack still loved her. She couldn't. I could see trouble brewing in this *ménage à trois*. It couldn't last for ever. If I was to be the catalyst who would destroy Jack's comfort, so be it. He had chosen one woman, he couldn't keep the other for himself also. But I wasn't going to abuse his hospitality and do it from inside his home. My honour wouldn't allow that. If I was to win Morvarid I must move out immediately.

CHAPTER VII

Maybe ten days, maybe two weeks had elapsed since I last saw Morvarid. I had been busy looking at Persian manuscripts in the Bodleian, but that was not the real reason. She had told me she did most of her research in the Bodleian, and I had been hoping to come across her there, but so far I had not seen her. Of course the 'Bodleian' consists of several buildings besides the Old Bodleian Library. She could be working in the Camera or in the New Bodleian (how stupid of me not to have asked her!). I could telephone her but she doesn't have her own phone. Who would answer? Maybe Joyce, maybe Jack. I don't feel like calling Jack after what he had told me in relation to my interest in Morvarid. Should I ask him 'May I speak to Morvarid, please?' I don't want to ask him! Or should I pay a courtesy visit to the Curtises to thank them for their hospitality? Hopefully Morvarid would show up and have tea with us. Indeed, she would probably be the one to make the tea. No. Jack would certainly guess the real reason for my visit. Write her a letter? What would I say in the letter? Ask her for tea? A very respectable Oxford tradition, boys and girls asking each other for tea in their rooms. Even Oriental girls had caught on it without fear or shyness. And then I would have to sit like an ass, waiting for her reply, not knowing whether or when she would accept my invitation. If I were to leave Oxford for Cambridge or London or any other place I could write her a long letter telling her how glad I had been to meet her, how I was hoping to see her again, a lot about friendship, with discreet allusions of something deeper than friendship developing between us. A 'meaningful relationship' used to be the term for it before it became a cliché. But we are in the same city. She is so near to me, and yet so far.

My predicament was solved for me quite unexpectedly. It was a hot September afternoon. I was standing in front of Blackwell's Bookshop looking at the display in the window. Most of the books were on sale and I cannot resist a book sale. I know I'll never have the time to read all the books I buy, but finding an interesting book at half price gives me a thrill similar to that experienced by a gambling addict when he wins a small sum of money. Suddenly I saw Morvarid coming down from the New Bodleian. She was wearing a green sari, which I took as an omen of good luck. She gave me a lovely smile:

'Hello, Sean! We haven't seen you for a long time.'

By 'we' I assumed she meant herself and her landlords. At that moment I wasn't prepared to explain to her the reason why I was avoiding their home. Not so suddenly.

'I have been somewhat busy,' I said, the common cliché. 'I shall explain to you some time, not just now,' I added. 'It's a bit complicated.' I thought I saw a mild expression of curiosity in her eyes. 'Perhaps we could go and have tea somewhere?' I felt too shy to invite her to tea in my new room on Pembroke Street, about ten or fifteen minutes' walking distance.

'Oh! I don't feel like sitting in a cafe,' she replied. 'I have got tired of sitting indoors on such a lovely day. I have come out to breathe some fresh air!'

'We could sit and talk in Exeter garden,' I suggested. 'It's very quiet there. Have you ever seen it?'

'No. But I'd like to.'

We crossed the Broad and passed by the back building of

Exeter College. 'Here was my window,' I pointed out to my companion. 'I had a view of Trinity chapel. I had been asked by the J.C.R. to allow it to be used as a secret entrance by undergraduates returning to College after midnight. Easier than climbing over the garden wall. Of course I couldn't refuse! So I had a lot of drunks coming into my room, looking for the door to the staircase and stumbling into my bedroom instead.'

We turned into the Turl. On our right we passed the Taj Mahal restaurant, an Oxford institution very popular with us undergraduate Orientalists. Perhaps later in the evening I would ask Morvarid to have dinner with me there? We continued along the Turl between Exeter and Jesus College. They seemed to be staring at each other like two mediæval fortresses with their battlemented roofs and square towers over their gates. Most Oxford colleges are built in the style of mediæval castles, a tradition harking to the wars between town and gown when the Colleges served as real fortresses, besieged by angry mobs. The bloodiest battle between scholars and citizens had taken place on St Scholastica's Day, 10 February 1355. The uneasy tension between town and gown still persists.

The gate to Exeter College was displaying the sign THIS COLLEGE IS NOW CLOSED TO VISITORS. We passed through unchallenged by the porter. I was wearing my blazer with Exeter crest and was prepared to shout my way in as a former undergraduate, not a mere tourist. To Morvarid, an Oxford student *in statu pupillari* it probably didn't occur to take any notice of the sign. We found ourselves in a large courtyard flanked on the right by the Late Gothic hall, on the left by the Victorian Gothic chapel, a sharp spire shooting from its steep roof. 'Have you ever seen our hall?' I asked Morvarid.

'No,' she answered, sounding slightly surprised at my question.

No wonder she was surprised. The question was silly from an Oxford point of view. When you are a student at Oxford you go to other colleges to attend lectures, to visit friends, to attend meetings of various societies, but you don't go just to admire their architecture. Just like the Gothic cathedrals of France or the Byzantine mosques of Istanbul. Marvellous, but if you've seen one, you've seen them all. At least this is how most of us used to feel, however much we may have loved Oxford architecture as a sum total. So why should Morvarid have come to have a look at Exeter if she had no particular business there?

But I love playing the tourist guide, whether it is in Old Montreal, in Old Quebec, in much older Oxford or in the really ancient cities of the Orient. I didn't get much chance in Iran. The locals either knew the place better than I did, or, most often, were not interested in old mosques and crumbling palaces. As to Europeans, I seldom met any outside Tehran. I was pleased Morvarid accepted to be shown Exeter Hall. The door was open. We found ourselves in a large Gothic structure with a high ceiling supported by black wooden beams. The stained glass windows allowed little sunlight inside. The furniture consisted of three rows of black wooden tables with austere benches without backs. At the end of the hall on a dais another table, just as austere, but with chairs instead of benches: the 'High Table' for the dons. In this hall I used to dine almost every evening during my first year in college, and very often during the following two years after I had moved into digs.

I looked at the large portraits adorning the walls, the portraits of long-dead distinguished scholars of the College in their crimson doctoral gowns.

'I had a fantasy during my undergraduate days to hide in this hall during the night,' I said to Morvarid. 'I wanted to talk to the ghosts of those men. I didn't really want to spend the night here except in my imagination. I had a poem in my mind, a rather anti-intellectual poem, denouncing the limitations of book learning. In that poem the portraits begin to speak and tell me about the futility of their lives spent among books and having missed the finer joys of life. I didn't despise learning as such, but I wanted to proclaim the superiority of the poet over the scholar, of passion over reason, of imagination over learning. Mind you, I was 19 years old at the time,' I added apologetically, implying that I had outgrown such nonsense. 'I think I was most influenced by Omar Khayyam who had been putting down his achievements as a scientist and praising wine-drinking instead. Even the idea of listening to the portraits of dead men talking had come to me from Khayyam's imaginary conversation with clay pots which had once been living men.'

'I would very much like to read your poem,' said Morvarid.

'Sorry' I answered. 'It was all in my head. I never put any of it on paper. I remember only two lines:

> I even studied Persian poetry
> While others gazed into Persians' dark eyes.'

In the semi-darkness of the hall I could say it and look into Morvarid's eyes without blushing.

We stepped into the sunlight outside. Still the tourist guide, I led my companion towards the Gothic chapel. 'I want to show you something which will interest you as a Zoroastrian,' I told her.

'Oh!' she exclaimed in surprise.

Exeter chapel, built by the Victorian architect Sir George

Gilbert Scott, is supposed to be a copy of the Sainte Chapelle in Paris. I have been several times to Paris, but I haven't seen the Sainte Chapelle. Anyway I like Gothic architecture, even Victorian Gothic. But the most famous object in Exeter chapel is the tapestry by William Morris depicting the homage of the Magi. Morvarid had heard of it, but had never seen it.

'Do you know?' I told her, 'The Magi were Zoroastrian priests. The word 'magus' comes from Old Persian *magush*, modern Persian *mogh*, although nowadays you seem to prefer the terms *maubed* or *dastoor*. Apparently they had seen a strange star in the sky and concluded it announced the birth of Sushians, so they came where the star led them to visit Him with their gifts.'

'Are you trying to tell me that Jesus Christ was Sushians?' the Zoroastrian girl asked me with a faint smile. 'Maybe He was, I don't know. The three Magi don't seem to have convinced many people when they returned to Iran and we knew nothing of their discovery. But I am not a strong Zoroastrian. I have a very strong faith in Ahura Mazda, but I don't believe Zoroastrianism is the only true religion, especially when it refuses to accept other people. It is more of a cultural or psychological attachment with me. Did you come to services here when you were living in College?'

'Goodness no!' I exclaimed. 'You forget that I am a Catholic. That was before Vatican II. I was afraid to come inside here! A synagogue, a mosque, a fire temple was OK, but a non-Catholic Christian church, absolutely out of bounds! Oh yes, we, I mean we Catholics, often paid nostalgic visits to mediæval English churches (not during services of course) which used to be Catholic 400 years ago, but this chapel had never been Catholic, so I didn't have the excuse. For Anglican members of the College, students and dons, attendance at services was still compulsory in my time, but the rule was no longer enforced.'

Again we stepped into the sunlight. I led Morvarid round the quadrangle past Palmer's Tower, once the entrance to the College and its only building surviving from the Middle Ages. We entered the dark passage past William Morris Room where two undergraduates had claimed to have seen the ghost of Exeter's most famous alumnus. At the end of the short passage we again stepped into sunlight, somewhat diluted by several trees. We were in the college garden. On our right the usual high wall enclosing all college gardens in Oxford, like the garden walls of Iran. Immediately on our left the Victorian Gothic college library, a fairly large building, but dwarfed by the adjacent Bodleian.

'Do you know,' I said to Morvarid, 'that Exeter is the only college which physically touches the Bodleian?'

'Must have been very convenient when you were living in college,' she answered laughing, 'especially on cold, rainy days.'

'Not so much,' I answered. 'There is no door connecting Exeter with the Bodleian, so I had to go via the Broad or Brasenose Lane.'

The garden ended in a mound, almost as high as the wall enclosing it. We climbed the steps to the top and sat on a bench overlooking Radcliffe Square. Bishop Heber's chestnut tree, not yet cut down, provided us with a comfortable shade.

'I have always loved this building,' I said to Morvarid, pointing to the dome of Radcliffe Camera, looming large in front of us.

'Didn't you tell me you appreciated Gothic better than neo-classical?' she asked me, slightly surprised.

'Yes,' I answered. 'As a rule I do, but I love a dome. It isn't really classical. The ancient Greeks didn't have it. A dome has a warmth which straight lines and right angles lack. It feels more baroque or rococo than classical. But, more important, it is the quintessence of Oriental architecture. How often I had gazed upon the Camera and imagined it to be the Aya Sofya, or the Umayyad Mosque in Damascus, or the Dome of the Rock in Jerusalem, or the shrine of Imam Reza in Mashhad, or the Taj Mahal . . . '

'In Xanadu did Kubla Khan a stately pleasure dome decree,' said Morvarid smiling.

'Yes! Exactly!' I exclaimed. 'Kubla Khan's palace probably had a Chinese style roof with corners turned up, yet Coleridge covers it with a dome. Why? Because the dome is the symbol of all Orient. He didn't care about accuracy. Even more strange is the presence of the Abyssinian maid. What was an Abyssinian girl doing in 13th century China? A war captive maybe? But the Mongols never got as far as Abyssinia. Luckily for the Abyssinians! So why not make her Mongol or Chinese? But Coleridge wasn't writing specifically about China, he wanted to evoke a mythical Orient with a mythical Oriental girl who could be Abyssinian or anything else. He was a poet, not an Orientalist scholar.'

'I must mention her in my thesis,' said Morvarid. 'Thank you for drawing my attention.'

'Talking about scholars,' I continued, 'see All Souls College over there?' I pointed across the square beyond the Camera. 'I used to go there twice a week to see my tutor, Professor Zaehner.'

'Zaehner?' exclaimed Morvarid. 'I have heard about him. He has written several books about our religion, but I haven't read any.'

'He could read the Avesta in the original as easily as he could read *The Times*,' I said. 'He was very popular with his fellow dons, who considered him an 'Oxford character'. I usually get along well with eccentrics, better than with square guys, hmm I mean fellows, but I always found him very cold and stiff. He told me at our first meeting: "I am not a professor of Persian. I am the Spalding Professor of Eastern Religions and Ethics." Implying that he was doing me a favour condescending to teach me. Our relations were always stiff and formal. He never became a father figure to me, as Pur-e Dawood later would in Tehran. I could never talk with him about my personal feelings towards the Orient or anything else. A confirmed bachelor living in college, I don't know if he had ever loved a woman, Oriental or other. And yet he did influence me greatly. We were reading a Middle Persian book called *Shkand Gumanik Vichar* ('Doubt Breaking Discourse') by a Zoroastrian author called Martan Farrukh.'

'I am afraid I have never heard of him,' said Morvarid.

'That's all right. He wasn't very famous,' I assured her. 'That book is as similar to modern Persian as Beowulf to modern English. And I was just learning Persian! It is a polemic against Muslims, Jews, Christians, Manichaeans and others. Zaehner told me he found Zoroastrianism the most rational religion in its explanation of the origin of evil, making the Devil, Ahriman, an independent, self-existing principle, not created by God. Answers the old question: Why doesn't God destroy evil once and for all? Why do bad things happen to good people? Nevertheless he didn't accept that Zoroastrianism was the true religion because, as he claimed it, it has failed the test of time; failed to convert the world. There are so few of you left. Seemed a strange argument to me, as if numbers should matter. Actually he was a convert to Catholicism, although this didn't draw the two of us together. Anyway, he had explained to me one point of Zoroastrian cosmology: Why are we here? The world is a place of struggle between the forces of good and evil. Before we were born God had asked our souls . . .'

'The *fravashis*,' interjected Morvarid.

'Yes, the *fravashis* . . . to take part in the struggle. So we are here as volunteers to fight Ahriman. If we get corrupted by him we shall end up in Hell which is his POW camp. If a misfortune not of our own doing happens to us we shouldn't blame God because all bad things, like illnesses, come from Ahriman. But the amount of evil in the universe is limited, so with each misfortune we suffer Ahriman loses a little of his ammunition, so to speak. Eventually he will exhaust it all. I don't think Zaehner, as a good Catholic, accepted all that, the prenatal existence of the soul or the implied limitation to God's omnipotence. I don't know if I do or ever did. But the idea of taking part in a cosmic struggle fascinated me. I saw myself as a fighter against Ahriman's injustice. That has often brought me into conflict with the authorities in the university and elsewhere. At McGill I am considered a troublemaker. They gave me the nickname the Tiger. I am lucky to have got tenure. Otherwise Ahriman's agents would have fired me in no time.'

'I see,' said Morvarid, smiling slightly, 'you do not always mind your own business.'

'Is that bad?'

'I don't know,' she answered. 'The British strongly believe in the virtue of minding one's own business, but I cannot help feeling that there is something cold and selfish in a lack of interest in other people.'

'All right.' I suddenly decided to take a gamble: 'Since you approve, or at least condone, interest in other people's business, may I ask you why have you taken lodgings with the Curtises?'

A cloud of suspicion seemed to pass across her face, but her voice was calm: 'I had to vacate my room in LMH and I preferred to stay with friends rather than with a strange landlady. What is unusual about that?'

'Seems strange to me that you should have accepted,' I said, 'but forgive me: it isn't my business.'

This time the suspicion was obvious, in her facial expression and in the tone of her voice: 'Why? Has Jack told you something about me?'

'He told me he had asked you to marry him, but you insisted to introduce him to your friend Joyce whom he had not met before. You had told him you thought Joyce would be more suitable for him as a wife. You gave him a faint hope that you might consider him if nothing came out of his meeting with Joyce. But he and Joyce fell for each other very fast and got married with your approval. This is what he has told me. I don't know how correct it is. He had quite a lot of whisky when he was telling me about it.'

'Yes, it is true,' she whispered.

'Well,' I said, 'I think Jack was a fool! (Of course I haven't told him that.) Oh yes, I understand that a man who is rejected by one girl is wise to find another. But all hope was not lost as far as he was concerned. You had told him that if he didn't want Joyce there was a possibility you might have accepted him, although you refused to promise anything. (At least that's the way he had related it to me.) The fool jumped for Joyce and failed the test. If I were in his place . . . If I had a glimmer of hope of winning you, I would have clung to that little bit of hope with all my strength! Sure, Joyce is a very fine woman, worthy of your friendship, but given the choice between the two of you, you are so much superior to her! Jack had a chance, however remote, of becoming the luckiest man in the world. He threw it away for a lesser good, just because it was easier to obtain.'

I was pleased with my words. I had hinted quite clearly to Morvarid that I loved her without actually spelling it out. Whenever I had loved a girl I had always felt an irresistible urge to let her know it. I had spoilt many a romance by a too hasty declaration of love. But that was the past. This time ostensibly I just paid the girl the compliment how great she was. She could continue to meet me and pretend to ignore the implication. After a moment of silence she spoke, very slowly, as if weighing her words:

'I understand that you have found my behaviour strange, even inconsistent, perhaps unfair to Jack. Yes, I did love him.' (I was pleased to hear her use the verb 'did love' in the past tense.) 'Now you are going to ask me why I did not accept when he asked me to marry him and tried to interest him in Joyce . . . '

'I understand,' I interjected. 'I know you Zoroastrians cannot marry outside your religion.'

'It wasn't exactly religion,' answered Morvarid. 'I have told you I am not a very strict Zoroastrian. I do believe in God, very strongly, but the Zoroastrian religion is just an identity symbol for me. Without it I don't belong anywhere. Call it psychological or cultural. You are an Orientalist, you should understand.'

'Yes, I understand' I answered. 'This is more or less how I feel about my Catholicism.'

'So,' continued Morvarid. 'I loved Jack, very deeply, but I was afraid to marry him. On the conscious level I could see no reason why I couldn't, but something deep, deep inside me held me back. I didn't know what to do. I wanted some other force, call it fate or whatever, to decide for me. I introduced Jack to Joyce. I don't know why I hadn't introduced him to her earlier, but it doesn't matter. You may be thinking that I was testing the strength of Jack's commitment to me. But it was myself I was putting to the test! Well, Jack and Joyce decided for me. I felt sad, but relieved at the same time. Perhaps it was best that way. Probably Jack is happier with an English girl than he would have been with me.'

Her revelation upset me: Her inhibition against marrying a Westerner had been a barrier against Jack, would almost certainly be a barrier against me. Courage, man: 'Almost' is the key word. Jack had found solace with another woman. Had he really? Trying to keep my voice calm I said:

'All of us experience contradictory feelings at times. I understand you so far. But, as I said earlier, I find it strange that you should have accepted to become Jack's tenant after . . . Anyway, it isn't my business. Maybe you prefer to close the subject?'

'I thought everything was over after Jack and Joyce got married,' Morvarid answered. 'I thought I could continue to be friends with both of them. I still loved Jack and wanted to be near him. I was happy that way. I was pleased to see Jack happy with Joyce. You don't think that I wanted to disturb their marriage, to play "the other woman", do you?'

'Goodness no!' I exclaimed. 'The idea never entered my head. You are a pure girl, a noble girl. But didn't you think that your constant presence . . . ?'

'Joyce didn't see me as a threat. It was she who had invited me, even insisted that I move in with them. And she knew what had passed between Jack and me.'

'Did it occur to you that deep, deep inside him Jack may still be loving you?'

She looked terrified. 'Why?' she exclaimed. 'What makes you think so? Has he told you something to that effect?'

'On the contrary,' I answered. 'He very much insisted he had done the right thing. Indeed, he insisted so strongly I felt he was trying to persuade himself, not me. As if he wasn't really sure.'

Morvarid regained her serenity: 'Oh Sean! You are imagining things! You are crediting me with some extraordinary powers which I am not even aware of.'

'Women do have powers which they are often unaware of,' I answered. 'It is part of your charm.' I was deliberately ambiguous as to whether by 'your charm' I meant women in general or her in particular.

'What should I do?' she asked with a helpless little girl look which I found particularly disarming. 'Should I move out? I hate looking for lodgings! No, I don't think I have to move out, at least not yet.' Suddenly her eyes flashed, the little girl look disappeared, and she continued in a firm voice with a slight trace of anger in it: 'But I shall make myself less available. Jack and Joyce have been taking me for granted. I really don't have time to cook for them almost every evening. Enough is enough. I have my thesis to work on. I had loved Jack once, but that is over now.'

'I felt Jack and Joyce had been exploiting you and I felt angry,' I said, 'but I couldn't say anything about it while I was being their guest. Anyway, if and when you decide to move out I shall be most pleased to help you search for lodgings and to move. You can count on me.'

Morvarid smiled: 'Thank you, I truly appreciate your offer, but I hope I won't have to move until I finish my thesis and get my D.Phil. Then I will really move out to go back to India.'

She didn't seem to take the possibility of staying in Oxford as a female don very seriously.

'Meanwhile, while we are both in Oxford,' I said, 'I hope I shall see you often. I know you are very busy with your thesis, but surely you will be able to spare some moments for me from time to time. I think we have a lot in common.'

'Yes, we do have very much in common,' admitted Morvarid quietly. 'But precisely because of it . . . maybe we shouldn't be seeing each other too often. The parting will be less painful. I do not wish to cause you pain.'

'When will that be? next summer?' I exclaimed. 'It's a long time from now. Until then . . . One hour with you is worth an eternity in Ahriman's Hell! I live for the present, not for the future.'

Morvarid did not look very convinced.

'Please don't worry on my account,' I said grimly. 'I have learnt some bitter lessons from life. When I experienced my first disappointment in love I thought the sky was going to fall down. But the sky didn't fall down, and I survived, "a sadder and a wiser man". The following time again I felt the sky was going to fall down. But I knew damn well it wouldn't. And it didn't. So, if we must part, if you go back to India, or if you just get tired of me and of my talk earlier than that, the sky will not fall down. I will survive to a bleak future in cold Canada, brightened by some memories of Oxford and of you. On the other hand, can I be sure? Maybe the sky will mercifully fall down this time. Maybe the earth will again get hit by an asteroid, like the one which had wiped out the dinosaurs 65 million years ago. Or, more likely, the Russians or the Americans will start a nuclear war and . . . '

'Oh Sean! You have a most morbid imagination!' exclaimed Morvarid. 'Please, don't talk like this.'

'I am prepared for the worst, but I can also dream of the best,' I replied. 'I can hope that my love for you will get reciprocated some time before your stay here is over. Of course, I have no right to demand of you to act against the principles of your religion. This is a matter for your conscience. For my part, I don't see anything morally wrong in loving you. On the contrary, my love for you is the best, the noblest thing there is about me. You may feel differently. But you tell me you had loved Jack. You had considered marrying him. You didn't say an absolute no to his proposal. That means you could love, even marry a man not of your religion and community.'

Morvarid sat silent for a few moments, then spoke slowly: 'My experience with Jack has taught me a lesson. Before he proposed to me the possibility of marrying a European, or any non-Parsee had never entered my mind. I had thought Jack and I were just good friends. He was an Indologist. I was an Indian. When he asked me to marry him I realized I loved him, but I was, afraid to . . . Well, I have explained it to you, you understand.'

'I understand,' I answered, 'that I have no right to demand your love, even less your hand in marriage, but could we be friends and see each other often, well, as often as you can spare the time from your thesis?'

Morvarid smiled: 'And do you think friendship between a man and a woman is possible without turning into a deeper involvement?'

'Of course not!' I answered. 'As Alfred de Vigny says, I don't remember the exact words:

Mais si Dieu près de lui t'a voulu mettre, ô femme,
Compagne délicate, sais-tu pourquoi?
C'est pour qu'il se regarde au miroir d'une autre âme . . .
'I forgot how it goes on.'

'Please! say it slowly!' exclaimed Morvarid. 'I have taken a course in French. Joyce had helped me. I can read it with a dictionary, but I cannot follow it when spoken fast.' (Maybe she just couldn't understand my Canadian pronunciation of French, acquired in the East End of Montreal?)

'It is beautiful,' she said after I had repeated to her the lines of Vigny's poem. 'I feel proud that you should call me the mirror of your soul. Yes, I would like to be your friend, although you know, friendship between a man and a girl is an idea which doesn't exist in my cultural background. Is it done in Iran?'

'But we are in Oxford, not in Iran,' I said, indirectly replying to her question that Iran was just like her country in that respect. 'And besides, you and Jack had been friends...'

'Yes, in all my innocence. In all my ignorance,' she corrected herself. 'I just didn't think how to label our relationship: call it friendship or what? Until he put me in a corner with his proposal. I have learnt my lesson: I must never, never accept the friendship of a man, Parsee or non-Parsee, Indian or European, unless I accept the possibility, however remote, that I may marry him some day.'

Her words filled me with dismay: Since I wasn't, due to my non-Parsee background, qualified to marry her, she wouldn't allow any friendship, any steady relationship between us. A chapter of my life was over like a beautiful dream. Turn the page, man, and prepare for the foggy Oxford autumn.

Her next utterance was like a ray of sunshine piercing through the blackness of my despair: 'I do value your friendship, Sean, and I don't want to, I cannot reject it. But to continue with you I must keep open the possibility, however slight, that I may marry you one day. I cannot promise anything yet, but I must be prepared for the eventuality.'

She took a small mirror out of her handbag and gazed into it intensely. I don't know if it had anything to do with the mirror metaphor in Vigny's poem. After a few minutes of silence she spoke slowly, still gazing into the mirror. She seemed to be speaking to herself rather than to me:

'You know, Sean, that Parsee girls, and Indian girls in general, seldom marry European men.' (Actually in Canada we use the term ''European' only for a person born in Europe, not for a Canadian of European origin, but this was irrelevant to her point, so I didn't interrupt.) 'Only very Westernized girls do.'

'Come on, girl!' I exclaimed. 'You are Westernized enough: almost a D.Phil.(Oxon.).'

Morvarid smiled: 'Intellectually perhaps. I know English literature much better than I know Gujarati or Hindi literature. I find it easier to write a letter in English than in Gujarati. But emotionally,' she continued in a serious tone, 'I am very Oriental, with all the inhibitions, conscious and subconscious (the subconscious ones are the worst) of an Oriental woman. If I am to embark on a steady friendship with a European man with the possibility of marriage, I must become someone else. No! I cannot and I don't want to become a different woman. But I can, I must change my persona, something superficial, but important to me. It will give me the illusion (I know it will be an illusion, but it doesn't matter) that I am a thoroughly Westernized Indian girl. I think I know what I'll do.'

She declined to tell me what it was that she would do to give herself the illusion that she was a thoroughly Westernized Indian girl. She told me, with a mysterious smile, that I would find out quite soon.

'It's getting a bit late,' I said. 'Could I invite you for dinner? May I invite you to the Taj Mahal? I don't understand the names of all those Indian dishes. You could help me decide what to choose.'

I wasn't being altogether truthful. I knew quite a lot about Indian food. Indian restaurants are as common and popular in England as Greek and Chinese restaurants in Montreal. Retired imperialist army colonels and civil servants often feel a strong nostalgia for India and Indian food and are their most frequent patrons. But the Taj Mahal caters mostly to Indian students longing for home or to Orientalists like Jack and myself. It was in the Taj that I had learnt the names of most, by no means all, Indian dishes during my undergraduate days. It is strange that the Taj Mahal, such a venerable Oxford institution, founded by the Bahadur family, doesn't have an entry in *The Encyclopaedia of Oxford*, not even a mention in the general entry on restaurants.

I was using a very old trick which I had used with other Oriental girls, pleading my ignorance of their culture in order to get them to accept my invitation to a dinner, a film, a concert, whatever. So I was hoping Morvarid would in the future accept to come and give me the cultural background of an Indian film, a concert of Indian music, a play by Tagore. Maybe we could take a day trip to London where she would be my very appreciated guide in the Indian art galleries of the Victoria Albert or the British Museum. Anyway, this time she most graciously accepted to be my guide through the complexities of the Taj Mahal menu.

We sat in a corner facing an intricately carved wooden model of a palace in Rajput style. The waiters seemed to know Morvarid. Of course they didn't know me; it had been such a long time since ... I recognized most of the dishes on the menu until I came across . . . *Sag gosht.*

'What's that?' I exclaimed.

'It is a spinach curry with meat' answered Morvarid. '*Gosht* means "meat" in Urdu. I think it is a Persian word.'

'Yes,' I said. 'It is pronounced *goosht* in Persian. But do you know what *sag* means?'

'*Sag* means "spinach" in Hindi,' said Morvarid with a somewhat puzzled look.

'In Persian *sag* means a "dog" ' I said. To a Persian the expression *sag goosht* or *goosht-e sag* would sound like "dog meat"!'

We both laughed, breaking the intense seriousness of our conversation in Exeter garden. Nevertheless I couldn't bring myself to try 'dog meat'. (I don't care much for spinach anyway.) Instead, very much against Morvarid's advice, I ordered a Madras chicken curry.

'Madras dishes are too hot even for us Bombay folk,' she said. 'You can be sure I will never cook Madras curry for you.'

I interpreted it that she may cook the much milder Bombay curry for me in the future. Wishful thinking!

She herself chose *dal* (lentil) curry which was the cheapest item on the menu. 'I love lentil!' she said smiling.

She graciously accepted my offer to walk her home, a long walk along St Giles and Banbury Road. She didn't invite me in, but that was understandable in view of what I had told her about Jack's perceived hostility towards my romantic interest in her. If Jack had been a stranger landlord it would have been none of his business. But he was my friend, she was supposed to be a friend of the couple, a most annoying situation.

I glanced furtively towards right and left. The street was empty. I kissed her on the cheek. She smiled: 'Good night, Sean. Thank you for the lovely dinner. I shall see you again soon.' Then she disappeared into the door of the Curtises' home. I stood there for several minutes, uncertain if it hadn't all been a dream. Then slowly I walked back to town.

CHAPTER VIII

I didn't see her again for what seemed to me a very long time. She telephoned me a couple of days afterwards telling me that she was going to London with Joyce for several days, perhaps for a week, to consult some books in the British Library. They would be staying with Joyce's aunt in South Kensington. She would give me another call when they are back. I dug my heels in the ground and tried to concentrate on the Persian manuscripts in the Bodleian. At last, after what seemed to me much longer than a week, the telephone rang.

'Hello, Sean!' said the sweet voice. 'I am back. Perhaps we could meet tomorrow afternoon if you are not too busy.'

'Why don't you come and have tea with me?' I asked her.

'I'd love to! I shall come about four. I have a little surprise for you' she added and giggled.

I bought a packet of Darjeeling tea and a small bottle of milk. I usually drink tea without milk, the Iranian way, but the Indians, like the British, can't conceive of tea without milk. And Morvarid was no exception. I also bought a fruit cake and some cookies, similar to the Iranian *shirini*. To make it fully traditional I should also have bought some thinly sliced white bread, butter and jam. Too messy and complicated! I was sure Morvarid wouldn't mind. I also tidied my room a little, arranging the papers on my desk into a neat little pile or hiding them in the drawers. I picked up the many books scattered all over the floor and with some difficulty found space for them on the overcrowded shelves. The landlady's maid who used to make my bed and clean the room every day didn't mind the booky mess, being well used to scholarly tenants.

On the following day long before four I sat waiting, my heart beating with impatience. I tried to read, but couldn't concentrate. I only recited two lines from Sa'adi's *Golestan*:

Farq ast miyan-e an ke yarash dar bar
Ba an ke do chashm-e entezarash bar dar.

There is a difference between one
whose companion is in his arms
And one whose two eyes
are fixed in expectation upon the door.

Four o'clock came and no sign of my expected guest. Five past four, ten past four, quarter past four. I felt like lighting a cigarette, but Morvarid had told me she hated the smell of tobacco, although Jack and Joyce both smoked heavily. At last a knock on the door! I sprung to my feet and rushed to open. 'Do come in!' I exclaimed even before I saw her.

I was almost thunderstruck by the transformation in her appearance. It is amazing how a woman's personality can change with a change of dress. During my stay in the Curtis home she used to wear a different sari almost every day. (This was part of the reason why I had found her so glamorous, as I had told Jack.) But now, for the first time, I saw her wearing European clothes. She was wearing a red beret on her head, a navy blue (or 'Oxford blue') trouser suit with a white blouse underneath. I marvelled at the wonderful slenderness of her figure. She seemed much taller than before. I guess the trousers made her look taller.

She took off her beret and I saw she had cut her hair short. There is something terribly dramatic when a beautiful girl cuts off her long hair, more dramatic than a change of costume. A girl can wear a skirt in the morning, slacks in the afternoon, a sari in the evening and change them at will. But if she cuts her hair it will take weeks if not months to grow again. If Morvarid had told me that she intended to cut her hair I am sure I would have begged her not to. But I was pleased with the result. She reminded me of Audrey Hepburn after she had cut off her long black hair in the film *Roman Holiday*. I understood that her change into European clothes and cutting her hair short was the surprise she had promised me.

In one way she looked to me more 'Oriental' than before in spite of her change into European clothes. I had always found her complexion much lighter than the average Indian, almost like a southern European. But against the white blouse her face appeared to me dark and mysterious, darker than I had hitherto felt. Although she used to wear saris of different colours she had never worn a white sari which is a sign of mourning in India. An optical illusion of course: A Spanish or Italian girl would likewise look darker in a white blouse.

Her lips were red, but not as deep red as Joyce's. It was the first time that I noticed her using lipstick. Or maybe the lipstick she had used before was so pale I had failed to notice it? I don't know. Likewise, she had painted her fingernails, but with a much lighter red than Joyce.

But her personality change did not consist merely of a different costume and hair style. Her smile was frank, without a trace of former shyness. It was no longer the enigmatic smile of the Sphynx or the Buddha. Nor was there a trace of shyness in her eyes. This unflinching gaze penetrated to the very depth of my soul. I remembered the Afghan love song: 'Your eyes are like a pair of loaded revolvers.'

She had never appeared to me as beautiful as now. But it was a different kind of beauty. She was no longer a Hindu goddess or a Byzantine icon. She was a real woman. I felt the burning but exquisite pain of desire rising within me. It was the first time that I desired her physically. I had loved her more deeply than any woman before, but any thought of desiring her physically had seemed like a sacrilege to me. I did have a strong physical desire for Joyce, mixed with a feeling of guilt because she was a married woman and because I felt I was betraying my true love, Morvarid. Well, not really. The beauty of those two women had belonged to two different spheres. But now Morvarid had shown me she could beat Joyce in her own field. There was something androgynous about Joyce's strong, athletic legs. But Morvarid, even in trousers (especially in trousers), was all woman, slender and delicate like a cypress swaying in the wind. I was trembling all over. I did not feel guilty about desiring her. I was going to marry her. Well, I was ready to marry her. If she refuses me in the end, it won't be my fault! But I did feel a sense of shyness and embarrassment.

'You look marvellous!' I thought I exclaimed, but the words came out of my mouth not louder than a whisper.

She smiled: 'You like me this way? I am pleased. I have given up the sari. From now on I shall always wear European clothes.' I was a little surprised at the emphasis she placed on the word 'always'.

I remembered reading as a teenager, when I was devouring all the travel books about the Orient I could find in the school library, a narrative translated from the Italian, entitled *Globetrotting* by one Antonio Zetto. The author had been hitch-hiking in Italian-occupied Libya when he was offered a ride in a car driven by a beautiful Arab girl, the daughter of a rich Bedouin sheikh. At that time even in Italy few women drove cars (Mussolini's daughter one of them) so she must have been a really emancipated girl. She took the author to the nearest town (I don't remember its name) and booked two adjacent rooms in the best available hotel. He was very much charmed by her until she went shopping and bought herself European clothes. 'To impress me more.' Instead, he was disgusted by her changed appearance. No doubt the Bedouin girl from the desert knew very little about European clothes and didn't know how to choose something which would look good on her. Zetto decided it was time to leave her and to continue with his globetrotting.

I thought Signor Zetto was an absolute idiot to abandon a beautiful girl because of such an easily repairable triviality. By his own (or his English translator's) description the girl looked 'lovely' in her Arab clothes. He could have told her: 'You know, *cara mia*, your beauty is a specifically Oriental type of beauty which shows best when you are wearing Arab dress.' Or he could have offered to go shopping with her and help her choose something in a better taste. Or rather, more to his taste. Of course it would have been a dress or a blouse and skirt. Women seldom wore trousers those days, apart from Katherine Hepburn and Marlene Dietrich. Apparently the girl had a crush on him and was trying to dress to please him, so she would have eagerly accepted either alternative. Of course Morvarid, who had lived in England among well-dressed Englishwomen ever since she had first come to Oxford as an undergraduate, would know how to choose tasteful English clothes, even if she had always worn Indian saris until now.

More relevant to me personally: during my undergraduate days I had often been told by Indian students that when an Indian girl discards her sari and puts on European clothes she indicates thereby her willingness to accept dates with European boys. (The term 'European' included of course

Canadians and Americans.) I thought I could detect a hint of warning in their advice: 'If you want to have an Indian girlfriend find yourself a liberated girl in European dress, but leave the respectable, traditional girls in saris to us.' Their advice may have been theoretically correct, but to me it was academic: all the Indian girls in Oxford used to wear saris. (Perhaps in red-brick universities some of them wore European clothes.) But now I thought: Maybe there was something to it, with Morvarid's firm announcement that she would 'always' wear European clothes from now on.

'Yes, I would like you to dress like this most of the time,' I said, my voice trembling. I said 'most of the time' as opposed to her 'always'. I felt I wanted her to wear a sari on special, dressy occasions. She didn't seem to notice the difference between her 'always' and my 'most of the time'.

'You are wearing pants...' I began.

'You don't say pants, you say trousers,' she corrected my North American English. 'You can say slacks, if it's a woman who is wearing them,' she added.

'Sorry! Shouldn't have forgotten my Oxford English,' I apologized. 'I have always felt that a beautiful girl looks most beautiful in pants, hmm, I mean slacks.'

'I have become aware of this quite soon after we met,' said Morvarid with what I thought was a mischievous twinkle in her eye. 'The way you were looking at Joyce's legs.'

I felt blood rushing into my cheeks: 'Do you think Joyce noticed?'

'Of course she did! She was pleased.'

'And her husband?'

'Jack likes men to admire his wife. Makes him feel proud of himself.'

I could see she was amused at my embarrassment.

'You know,' I said by way of apology, 'during my undergraduate days here very few girls used to wear slacks, except for sports. Those who wore trousers every day were very sophisticated girls, poetesses or artists. The boys used to go crazy about them! I also found them fascinating: I thought every girl who wore slacks had some mysterious reason for it: She was a Joan of Arc or a George Sand. But it worried me: I felt divided between two apparently conflicting feminine ideals: the woman in trousers and the Oriental woman. Somehow it didn't occur to me that the Oriental woman could also wear trousers and beat the Western enchantress at her own game.'

'Joyce identifies with George Sand,' answered Morvarid. 'But I am not George Sand and even less Joan of Arc. I don't want to be burnt! Nor can I claim to be a poetess or an artist,' she continued, 'although I love poetry, especially English poetry, and I appreciate art. But times have changed. All Oxford girls are wearing slacks now, even the younger dons. I just follow the fashion.'

Of course by 'all Oxford girls' she meant the University girls. The city girls and whatever they wore were not taken into consideration. To her, as to (almost) all faculty and students the City was a different world, outside the ivory tower. It was almost like apartheid, or like the 'Two Solitudes' of English and French Montreal.

'And you have cut your hair,' I said with a slight tone of reproach.

Her eyes flashed with a look of defiance: 'It was taking too much of my time: combing it, washing it, drying it, setting it . . . You had asked me to see you often, which I am looking very much forward to, but I have to find time for it. I can't take time off my thesis!' she said almost angrily. 'I had to sacrifice something for the sake of our friendship. If you like, I shall grow it again after I get my D.Phil. But,' she added, walking towards the mirror above my mantelpiece, 'I like myself like this. It is called Eton crop. You know, in India when a girl cuts her hair short, it is considered a gesture of rebellion, an act of liberation, most important, a declaration that she would choose for herself the man she would marry, instead of her parents choosing him for her.'

'You look good! I like you this way; I prefer you this way,' I said in all sincerity, kissing the nape of her neck, something I couldn't have done easily when she wore her hair long. 'I wish you had let me cut your hair for you!' Somehow I felt that the act of cutting off her long hair would have been a symbolic way of taking possession of her, almost like an engagement ritual.

'You?' she answered laughing. 'Are you a women's hairdresser? You would have made a real mess of it!'

'You have said you would always wear slacks from now on . . . ' I began.

'I said I would always wear European clothes,' she corrected me. 'I can wear trousers most of the time if it pleases you, but I am not a tomboy like Joyce. I have bought some very feminine-looking blouses at Harrod's, most of them made in India, of Indian cotton to wear with my trousers. You will like that, won't you?' she smiled coquettishly. 'But I can't wear trousers all the time in Oxford. I have to wear my gown on some occasions, and you know women are not permitted to wear trousers with academic dress. So I shall have to wear a skirt. Besides, we are in England, not in Canada. Do girls in Canada wear trousers all the time?'

'McGill students do. Some girls had told me they didn't even possess a skirt.'

'Well, I am not a Canadian girl,' said Morvarid testily. 'We are more conservative here.' (It struck me how strongly she had come to identify with England, or at least with Oxford, to use the pronoun 'we'.) 'I can't go to formal parties wearing slacks, although Joyce does. She just hates wearing a dress or skirt. But I shall wear a dress and a hat. You will see. I shall take you along with me. I want you to meet all my friends.'

'You could wear a sari for dressy occasions,' I suggested.

Again I saw a lightning flash in her eyes.

'I shall never wear a sari again!' she exclaimed with a vehemence which I found most puzzling. 'I have told you. I shall always wear European clothes. Unless,' she added, her voice faltering, 'our friendship breaks down and we have to part. Oh, I hope this will not happen!'

I was beginning to see the connection between her consent to accept steady dating with me and her decision to wear European dress. Presumably she didn't want to be regularly seen in public with a Western boy while wearing a sari. I felt a sharp pang of regret. I found her more approachable and, yes, more sexy in Western clothes, but I thought I would have liked her to wear a sari from time to time, my mysterious Oriental princess.

'I may wear a sari once again for you,' she said, as if divining my thoughts. 'Just once, for a very special occasion. That red one, with the gold-embroidered border which you had said you liked best. Doesn't have to be white, does it? But, I have to repeat it to you again, I cannot promise you anything yet.'

'You may find my decision to discard the sari somewhat puzzling,' she continued after a moment of silence. 'I shall try to explain it to you. Last time, in Exeter garden you had asked for my friendship. You had told me you loved me, you had called me the mirror of your soul. I was deeply, deeply moved by that. I felt I couldn't reject your friendship. But I told you I couldn't accept steady friendship with a man unless I was prepared for the possibility of marrying him. I told you that Parsee girls, and Indian girls in general, seldom marry European men. Only very Westernized girls do. But I am very Oriental for all my English education. There is something lurking in my subconscious which makes me afraid to marry a Western man. It isn't religious, it is more cultural. But I have found a way to overcome that fear and even eliminate it altogether. I had to convince my subconscious that I am a truly Westernized Indian girl. I had to change my persona in a dramatic, if superficial way. I decided to give up the sari and wear European dress. But the change had to be complete. It wouldn't do to wear slacks today and a sari tomorrow. Only in Western clothes do I feel like a liberated woman, free to love and possibly marry a Western man.

'I know, Sean,' she continued, 'you are a romantic Orientalist. You would like to marry a completely Oriental girl, a fairy tale princess like Lalla Rookh. But that is impossible. Every Oriental woman who has married a Western man has had to give up some aspect of her heritage. It could be something very tiny and insignificant, it could be something very important. In my case it will be my religion. Is Oriental dress so important to you? After all I am a Parsee, meaning a Persian. Don't Persian women in Iran wear European clothes?'

'In the cities they do.'

'There you are! You can think of me as a Persian, which I am by ancestry, although I am sure I have some Hindu blood in me. I think I can offer you some of my Oriental culture even if I don't wear a sari. I shall decorate your home to look really Oriental; I shall cook Indian curry for you; I shall teach you Gujarati if you are still interested; I shall sing Gujarati and

Hindi songs for you. If we have children I shall speak Gujarati to them. Won't that make me Oriental enough in your eyes, even without a sari? But I must repeat to you again, I cannot give you a promise yet. We are going about it the Western way. In India a marriage is an arrangement between two families. That was part of the reason why I escaped to England. In the West a boy and a girl go 'dating' until they get to know each other well enough . . . '

'I know you well enough!' I exclaimed. 'I could marry you tomorrow!'

'You are a man,' answered Morvarid calmly. 'You men make decisions quickly without thinking of the risks involved, but I am a woman even if I am wearing trousers.' She smiled. 'We women need time to make the most important decision of our life. Now, if we do get married, have you considered how and where? A Zoroastrian marriage is out of the question, so it will have to be either a civil marriage or in your Roman Catholic Church. Jack and Joyce had a civil marriage although they are both nominal Anglicans, but I would feel more at ease if it is blessed by a religious rite, even if it isn't mine. Your God and our Ahura Mazda is the same, even if we call Him by different names.'

'I know I can't become a Zoroastrian any more than Professor Pur-e Dawood could,' I said. 'But you can become a Catholic. After all there are more Catholics than Parsees in India. So it won't make you any less Indian.'

'True. I could have been born a Catholic. From Goa or from Kerala. It would have made things easier for us. I wouldn't have to change my persona to convince myself that it is all right for me to marry an Irish Catholic from Canada. I could have continued wearing a sari without inhibition. But,' she added, her eye twinkling mischievously, 'I would probably have had a dark skin like the Goans and the Keralans and you wouldn't have wanted to marry me.'

'You do me wrong!' I almost shouted, piqued by this accusation of racism, even if said in jest. 'I wouldn't want your face any darker or lighter than it is, but in general I find dark-skinned women beautiful. Like Ajanta paintings.'

'Calm down, Sean!' she answered laughing. 'I was teasing you. Now, you have invited me for tea. Let us have some tea.'

In all this excitement I had forgotten my obligations as a host. I felt embarrassed, a fact which Morvarid seemed to find amusing.

'Just put the water to boil, I'll do the rest,' she commanded. 'Do you have a pot and two cups? Good! Where is your tea? Darjeeling! Excellent!'

Over the tea our conversation became less serious. I thought I could now take my turn and tease her a little:

'You had told me you and Joyce were going to London to the British Library, but apparently you had gone to buy clothes at Harrod's.'

Morvarid's eyes flashed in anger:

'I did not lie to you! I am a Zoroastrian! I never lie!'

I knew her boast was not vain. While Shi'a Persians tend to be tolerant of harmless lies which hurt no one and which may even be a form of poetic self-expression, the same cannot be said of the Zoroastrians, stern adherence to truth under all circumstances being the central principle of their religion.

'Joyce and I did have to go to the British Library,' she continued by way of explanation. 'On top of that I had to go to India Office Library to see some personal papers of Meadows Taylor. This, and shopping for clothes made quite a hectic week, I tell you. I was grateful to Joyce to come with me to

Harrod's and other shops. I don't know why the silly girl was giggling all the time.'

Colonel Philip Meadows Taylor was an officer in the Army of the East India Company. Unlike most British imperialists he strongly approved of intermarriage between British and Indians, hoping that the amalgamation of the two races would perpetuate British rule in India. His own Anglo-Indian wife was, he claimed, a descendant of Mughal Emperors on her mother's side. Although his literary talent was not equal to Kipling's his knowledge of and sympathy for Indians was definitely greater. I had first heard about him from Jack to whom he was a hero. He may have been a minor, now forgotten novelist, but of course for Morvarid's thesis he was important.

After we finished our tea Morvarid wanted to wash the tea cups. With some difficulty I dissuaded her, pointing out that my landlady's maid would do it the following day. She was getting good tips from me. We sat next to each other on a small couch.

'I would have liked to wear high heels with my slacks,' said Morvarid as I was staring at her trousered legs. 'But my feet are very moody. I always have problems finding comfortable shoes. I have several pairs of high heels, but I shall wear them only when I must, on very dressy occasions, when I have to wear a skirt. Hope you don't mind.'

It occurred to me with a slight embarrassment that I hadn't noticed what kind of shoes she had been wearing with her saris.

'You look just marvellous the way you are, high heels or no high heels,' I said. 'You looked beautiful in a sari, but I prefer you like this. You said European clothes give you the illusion of being a Westernized Oriental woman. Your changed appearance gives me an illusion too. I feel all the barriers between us have crumbled down. I have no more apprehension of the future. You are my girl. I feel we shall never be parted from each other.'

'But I have told you I cannot promise you anything yet. We have known each other for such a short time . . . ' said Morvarid in a somewhat alarmed voice.

'So what?' I answered. 'I know it's an illusion, but it's a heavenly illusion. You have given me such happiness as I have never known in my life. Until this afternoon I knew I loved you more than I had ever loved any woman, but only now, when I saw the change in you I realized it had been a Manichaean sort of love.'

'Manichaean?' Morvarid looked puzzled. 'The Manichaeans were a religious sect in ancient Iran, but this is all I know about them. Tell me about them. Did they have some special ideas about love?'

'Their founder, the prophet Mani, was born in Iraq in the third century AD,' I began, ever an academic, even in such a romantic situation. Girls less intellectual than Morvarid had either laughed at my schoolmasterly pedantry or just found it plain boring. 'He acknowledged Zarathushtra, Jesus and the Buddha as earlier prophets, but claimed their teaching had been distorted. Like Zarathushtra he believed in two independent Creators, Ahura Mazda and Ahriman, but, unlike Zarathushtra, he preached that all matter was the creation of Ahriman, therefore evil. His religion spread over a huge area from France to China. St Augustine, the one from North Africa, not the one from Canterbury, had been a Manichaean before his conversion to Catholicism. They were persecuted everywhere except in China and Central Asia. They regarded sex as evil, not even a necessary evil, a creation of Ahriman.

Celibacy was the only way to save one's soul. Like the Shakers in 19th century America. Yet, I would say, they couldn't have been indifferent to love and beauty, especially the beauty of women. In the caves of Central Asia which had served as their monasteries have been found manuscript books with wonderful miniature paintings supposedly depicting angels (there must be good reproductions in the Ashmolean) but the angels look like beautiful women dressed in garments very similar to your sari. They, I mean the Manichaeans, are supposed to have had an influence on other religions, including Christianity. There is a famous icon by the Russian painter, Andrei Rublov, supposedly representing the Holy Trinity. It shows three rather dark women in robes similar to saris. Rublov was an Orthodox monk, committed to celibacy. Yet, in trying to depict the supreme Beauty he had to use the imagery of three women. Such was my love for you until this afternoon. No, it wasn't 'platonic'. It was too intense for that. You were to me (and you still are!) the ideal of beauty and love. But there was no physical desire in my love for you. The thought of it seemed like a sacrilege. You were too sacred for that. But the sensual side of me couldn't be suppressed and I looked at Joyce's trousered legs and I felt guilty, guilty because she was a married woman, guilty because I felt I was being disloyal to you . . . But now, when I saw you in European clothes everything has changed. I love you as a man loves a woman. You know what I mean.'

'I think I do,' she whispered. 'Maybe I shouldn't wear provocative European clothes in front of you. Or at least I shouldn't wear trousers. I don't want to be a temptress.'

'Too late now!' I said wistfully. 'Won't make a difference. I have seen how marvellous you look in trousers and it has printed an indelible image on my memory, whatever you may decide to wear from tomorrow on. But is it necessarily bad? You are a Zoroastrian, not a Manichaean. You acknowledge sensual love to have been created by Ahura Mazda, not by Ahriman. This is what religious marriage is for. Rest assured: I swear to you by my Catholic faith (it has a grip on me in a childish sort of way, Vatican II or no Vatican II) that, however strongly I want you, I shall not try to take you until we are married, whatever kind of marriage you want us to have. I respect you too much to want otherwise. But I must marry you! I will marry you! My conscience is clear.'

Morvarid smiled: 'I understand you, Sean. You are a man, not an angel. And I am not an angel either. I am a woman. And I expect to be loved like a woman when I get married to you ... I mean, if I get married to you,' she quickly corrected herself.

'But meanwhile ... could you give me ... ' I began. I put my arm round her and gently drew her towards me. I gazed into her eyes, dark and deep like the water wells in the Baluchistan Desert. And I had the sensation of falling headlong into a dark deep well. Down, down I went until my lips met hers in a long, long kiss. I felt intoxicated. The taste of her lips reminded me somehow of the strong red wine I had been offered by my Zoroastrian hosts in Kerman. A feeling of immense joy came upon me. I felt I had won her love, however hesitant she may still be in giving me a formal 'yes'.

CHAPTER IX

The weeks, the months that followed were among the happiest in my life. We saw each other often. Whenever she told me she was too busy to see me because she wanted to finish a chapter in her thesis to show it to her supervisor I knew she was speaking the truth, that it was not an excuse to be rid of me. We usually fixed our dates by telephone. She used to call me more often than I called her. The reason was of course Jack. Whenever Joyce answered the telephone she was always very friendly and charming, but her husband, while never exactly impolite, was always very abrupt. 'May I speak to Morvarid, please?' He would summon her if she was in or tell me curtly he would inform her of my call, which, to be fair to him, he always did. This made me hesitant to call her and she understood it. I didn't advise her to get her own telephone because I felt she should instead look for lodgings elsewhere, something she was most reluctant to do.

We usually met in my room on Pembroke Street. During those last days of summer we would take a walk round Christ Church Meadow and by the river. College crews were training for the Torpids.

'You used to row when you were an undergraduate, didn't you?' Morvarid asked me.

'Yes' I said proudly. I rowed in Exeter Eight. But do you know what made me join the Boat Club in the first place?' I asked her in a more pensive mood. 'I liked the name of the river: Isis. Isis was the Egyptian goddess of the moon. I found the name romantic. But more important: Do you remember the college barges?'

Morvarid looked puzzled: 'Barges?'

'They must have dismantled them before your time,' I explained. 'Each college boat club used to have its own wooden barge moored to the bank. Its main purpose was to serve as a changing room, but it also had a sitting-room in front where we could warm ourselves with hot tea after rowing in winter. The roof of the barge formed a deck from which spectators could watch the race and cheer the College boat. Those barges were most beautifully carved, like Portuguese caravels sailing for the Indies. I just loved them! Later, when I was in Tehran I heard that it was decided to scrap them (probably it was too expensive to keep wood from rotting in the water) and to move the crews into drab boat houses. More practical no doubt, but . . .

'Just as my suede jacket and slacks are more practical than a sari for walking with you along the windy river bank,' said Morvarid laughing. 'Oh Sean! You are an impossible romantic with your nostalgia for everything old!'

*   *   *

The autumn rains put an end to our strolls by the river and drove us into cafes. The new kind of cafe serving espresso and capuccino had made its appearance in Oxford when I was an undergraduate and became very popular with the so-called 'arties' who considered capuccino more sophisticated than the traditional English tea.

We usually had dinner at the Taj Mahal, sometimes at other restaurants. Morvarid almost always used to choose the cheapest item on the menu, claiming that this was what she liked best. Maybe she did.

She seldom accepted an invitation to a film, pointing out that it would be a waste of time. We would have to sit watching the film, unable to talk to each other. And she considered talking the most important part of our relationship, claiming it would enable us to get to know each other and make sure we really were meant for each other. My mind was of course made up but I enjoyed talking to her. She made an exception for films made from English literary classics like Jane Austen or E.M. Forster.

With a delightful feminine lack of logic she eagerly accepted invitations to concerts in Holywell Music Room where we had to sit very quiet without so much as a whisper. She admitted to me that, although she appreciated Hindustani music, she liked classical Western music better. Indeed, she had taught me how to appreciate Western music. As a boy I had never cared for music of any kind, except perhaps for the bagpipes I had heard in Nova Scotia. My parents and teachers said I had no musical ear. Until I heard some Arabic music, mostly Lebanese pop songs, on the ethnic radio station in Montreal. To me it was the most beautiful music I had ever heard! I sat enchanted, listening, my eyes closed. I had discovered a love of music in myself. I came to love all Oriental music, Middle Eastern, Indian, even Japanese, and my love of Oriental music has played no small part in my fascination with the Orient. In European music I cared only for the music of Greece and the Balkans which is more Middle Eastern than European or for the flamenco music of Spain which sounds more Arabic than anything. With Morvarid I learned to appreciate classical Western music, although Oriental music is still my preference. Most of all I love Oriental themes in European music, such as the Turkish tunes in Tchaikovsky's *Slavonic March* or the Japanese songs in Puccini's *Madama*

Butterfly. I think Morvarid with her dual cultural background would agree with me.

*   *   *

True to her decision Morvarid always wore European clothes. Most of the time she wore trousers. She had bought many pairs, different colours, different styles, some very narrow, some as wide as, well, 'slacks'. I liked her best in jeans, but she was most reluctant to wear them in downtown Oxford. They were all right for the home or for strolling in Christ Church Meadow, but not for the Bodleian reading room or the sophisticated cafes. Only 'low class' girls wore jeans everywhere. 'Low class' or not, jeans seemed to me the very antithesis of a sari, and this contrast added to my feeling of fascination with her new appearance.

Occasionally she would wear a skirt. Although I found her more attractive, or rather (let me call a spade a spade!) more sexy in trousers I liked to see her in a skirt for a change. With dress or skirt she would often wear a broad-brimmed hat which cast a dark shadow on her face. To a Middle Eastern or Indian woman a hat is a symbol of Westernization (Reza Shah had unsuccessfully tried to make Iranian women wear hats as a sign of modernity), yet it can give her an air of mystery as much as an Oriental veil. I loved to see her in a hat! I remembered the times when she used to wear a sari, especially that evening when I first met her and was overwhelmed by her shy Oriental charm or that afternoon in Exeter garden when we first spoke of friendship and of love, with a feeling of nostalgia which added a bitter-sweet tinge of melancholy to my happiness. But I was glad she was wearing European clothes. It gave me the illusion, no, not the illusion, the certainty (whatever she may have said about our not knowing each other well enough) that she was my girl and I was going to marry her. Her European dress looked to me like an engagement ring. (When I suggested buying her a ring she very firmly told me not to at this stage.) Nevertheless she wanted to continue wearing something Indian. The colourful blouses she liked to wear with her slacks were for the most part imported from India. They were cut in European style, but the material looked very Oriental with flowery or geometrical motives. Some of the designs looked very Iranian. Maybe she wanted to support the Indian cotton industry as an act of expiation for considering marriage to a foreigner? Later, when the weather cooled she would wear a thick Kashmir sweater on top of her blouse.

Out of curiosity I asked her whether she had ever worn European clothes before she met me. To my surprise she answered yes. She had attended an English girls' school in Bombay. Although the school was run by the Anglican Church the strictest respect was paid to the students' religion, Hindu, Muslim, Zoroastrian, Sikh, Jain, Catholic or other. No attempt was made to convert them. The school had given Morvarid a love of English literature, but, unlike similar establishments in England, no training in any sports. A concession to local culture: Indian parents were very anxious to give their daughters an English education, but disapproved of sports for girls. (Their brothers of course were playing cricket in their school.) The girls wore the usual English schoolgirl uniform consisting of a pinafore dress with a necktie and a sun hat. Some Muslim girls used to wear a white scarf instead of a hat.

In Oxford she had always worn a sari, first with the short undergraduate gown, then with a BA gown and finally with a MA gown over it. Except for exams and degree taking ceremonies when 'full academic dress' was obligatory. With full academic dress all male members of the University, from the Chancellor to freshman undergraduate, were required to wear a black suit with a white shirt and a white bow tie. Women members of the University wore a black jacket and skirt with a white blouse. Most Indian girls would wear a black sari.

'I didn't want to wear a black sari,' Morvarid told me. 'Didn't want to look like a nun. So I bought myself a black jacket and skirt like the English girls. But I have worn it only for those occasions. I hope you will see me wearing it in the Sheldonian when I take my D.Phil. degree!'

Had she ever worn trousers? No, not until she decided to permanently wear European clothes. She admitted with a giggle that she had felt a little self-conscious at first, but very soon came to appreciate the comfort and freedom of movement the slacks gave her.

'I wish all Indian girls in Oxford would give up their attachment to the sari and start wearing slacks like other Oxford girls!' she sighed wistfully. 'I don't want to be the only one.'

'Someone had to set the precedent,' I consoled her. 'You may become the fashion setter.'

'You think they'll follow me? You're being very optimistic!' she laughed.

While the sight of her in blouse and trousers aroused the most burning desire in me, I experienced a certain masochistic pleasure precisely at my not being allowed to quench that fire. It was like holding a glass of brandy and feeling the delicious fragrance without touching it with my lips; or like contemplating the architecture of a beautiful castle before rushing to enter its closed door. My burning pain was made bearable, pleasurable even, by the certain knowledge that one day I would marry my desire, pull down her defences and penetrate the door of the no longer forbidden castle.

Meanwhile, in the privacy of my room at Pembroke Street I was permitted all sorts of caresses, but I had to learn how far I could go. Once, when I forgot myself in my excitement I was given a rude awakening:

'Stop it, Sean! If you cannot control yourself maybe I should stop this Westernized woman experiment and go back to wearing a sari like a good, conservative Indian girl.'

I would have liked to see her in a sari again but I understood the implication. I learned my lesson.

*　　*　　*

Sometimes we discussed our future.

'I had taken it for granted that I would return to India after I get my D.Phil.' Morvarid was telling me. 'Elizabeth says . . . '

'Who is Elizabeth? Oh yes, Elizabeth Jameson, your supervisor of course. Sorry. Go on.'

'Elizabeth says she can secure for me a fellowship at LMH with the position of a junior don, but I haven't been taking her seriously.'

'In Canada, with a D.Phil. from Oxford the English Department at McGill will just grab you!' I exclaimed. 'You will become a full professor before I move from assistant to associate! Although,' I added smiling, 'I wouldn't mind if you just stay at home, decorate the place to look Oriental, cook Indian curry for me and, most important, love me when I come back tired from work.'

'Male chauvinist!'

'Thank you for not calling me a male chauvinist pig!'

'Joyce would have called you just that.'

We also talked about a possible visit to India where I would be introduced to her family. Of course I found the idea very exciting.

'And will you wear a sari in India?' I asked half hopefully. Since she would be my wife, the sari would no longer symbolize a barrier between us.

'Not if I go with you as your wife. I shall wear a summer dress and a sun hat. My family will have to accept it. I may even wear white cotton slacks whenever I can permit myself to be more casual. You will like that, won't you?' She smiled coquettishly.

We had by now agreed that when we would marry (if we would marry, as she insisted on putting it) we would take a Catholic marriage, a Zoroastrian marriage being out of the question. She rationalized her eventual conversion to Catholicism with the theory that Jesus Christ, who had received the visit of three Zoroastrian priests, may really have been Sushians, the Saviour foretold by Zarathushtra. She began coming with me to the Sunday Mass at the Newman Chapel, located in the 'Old Palace' about a hundred yards from my Pembroke Street lodgings. In the confusion following Vatican II I had become a somewhat neglectful church-goer, although I had never lost my faith in God. Since I met Morvarid however I began to go to church regularly, praying fervently: 'Oh God or Ahura Mazda, whatever is Thy name, do let me have this girl! Only with her at my side can I lead the life of good thoughts, good words, good deeds which is Thy command in the Gospels and in the Avesta.'

To Morvarid the most interesting aspect of the Newman Chapel were the sermons of Father Pereira, a Jesuit from Goa, now at Campion Hall. He was writing a D.Phil. thesis about the concept of 'just war' in the Bhagavad-Gita and Thomas Aquinas. He was also helping as assistant chaplain at the

Newman. Although he spoke English with a strong Indian intonation his sermons were very popular with students and dons, even with many non-Catholics. He was very enthusiastic about the South American liberation theology and railed against Western imperialism and the war in Vietnam, obviously not a 'just war' by either the Gita's or Aquinas's criteria. He gave me the confidence to divulge to him my love interest in a non-Catholic, indeed a non-Christian girl.

'Morvarid Cama?' he repeated the name, his dark South Indian face breaking into a smile. 'A very fine girl! A very fine girl indeed!' (He knew all the Indian students in Oxford, Christian and non-Christian.) 'You'll be a very lucky man if you can win her, my friend. . . . Yes, of course Our Lord Jesus Christ was the Sushians foretold by Zarathushtra. But you must not try to convert her. Only the Holy Ghost can do that. I shall pray for both of you.'

*　　*　　*

From time to time Morvarid would invite me for tea in the Curtis home. I was reluctant to go but couldn't resist her insistence. The tea which she would offer me was always more elaborate than whatever I offered her. It was more like what the British call 'high tea', a full meal in itself. Beside the usual fruit cake there were all sorts of sandwiches, buttered scones with jam and some other goodies. The tea itself was prepared in the Indian manner, with hot milk and spices. Both Morvarid and Joyce played the part of hostesses. Joyce was most charming, and, as usual, a most interesting conversationalist. Her husband however would greet me curtly:

'Hello, Sean! How are you? I trust you are doing well. Excuse me, I have lots of work by all those dumb undergraduates to correct.'

And he would shut himself in his study. I thought I could detect a note of sarcasm in his 'I trust you are doing well'. The British, like the Persians, have the ability of saying sarcastic things with a straight innocent face as if they had said nothing. But maybe he wasn't being sarcastic. Maybe I was over-sensitive. I felt he had changed since our undergraduate days. We had become estranged from each other. Or maybe it was I who had changed? Or both of us? Our friendship was no longer what it had been. I remembered the stanza from Sir Richard Burton's *Kasidah*:

> 'Friends of my youth, a last adieu!
>   haply some day we meet again;
> Yet ne'er the self-same men shall meet;
>   the years shall make us other men.'

Now I was able to compare the beauty of the two women as they sat next to each other. When Morvarid wore the sari her beauty seemed to belong to an entirely different dimension from Joyce's. But now, seeing both of them dressed more or less alike, in blouse and slacks, I definitely found Morvarid the more beautiful of the two. Joyce was all European, all sensual. Morvarid looked equally sensual in her European clothes, but her delicate features, her dark eyes, her black (albeit short) hair retained all the mystery of the East. Hair dyed blonde may look very sexy, but I find black hair more beautiful.

Morvarid was determined that I should meet her friends. She had kept somewhat aloof from the Oxford Indian community and wasn't a member of Oxford Majlis. Nevertheless she had three close friends among the Indian girls. Shortly after her Westernizing transformation she invited them and myself for tea. Fortunately Jack was out. Joyce was, as usual, a most gracious co-hostess. Two of the girls wore saris, the third, a pretty girl with a complexion as fair as Morvarid's, wore a costume called *shalvar o kamees*, consisting of a short flowery dress worn over wide white trousers, with a white silk shawl draped over her shoulders, a symbolic veil which could be drawn over the head if necessary. She could recite some Persian poetry which she had learnt in an Islamic girls' school in Kashmir. Of course she pronounced it according to the traditional Indian pronunciation of Persian, closer to the Afghan or Tajik than to Iranian. Morvarid introduced me to them as 'my friend from Canada'.

The three girls were fascinated by Morvarid's European clothes and plied her with questions: Where did she buy them? how much did she pay? how did she know what exactly to select? etc., etc., etc. They looked at her with admiration mixed with awe, as if she had done something extremely daring, like hitch-hiking across Europe with a rucksack on her back. Not satisfied with admiring the trouser suit she was wearing, they demanded to see the rest of her newly acquired wardrobe. She took them to her room leaving Joyce to entertain me. For about ten or fifteen minutes I could hear loud giggles coming from upstairs.

'Silly girls!' Morvarid told me afterwards. 'They wanted to try my clothes on and come down to show themselves to you. I did not let them. But really they will never dare to wear European clothes in public. And none of them will accept a date with or marry a European boy. No Hindu girl will marry you. Waseema may, if you become a Muslim.'

'I might have become a Muslim if you were one,' I answered, 'but it is you whom I want to marry, not Waseema or anyone else.'

'I don't mean you personally, you idiot!' answered Morvarid, sounding half angry half amused. 'I mean any European boy.'

In order to meet more of her friends she used to take me along with her to sherry parties she was invited to in various colleges and dons' homes. On those occasions she would wear a large, richly embroidered Kashmir shawl over her Harrod's dress. It made her look mysterious and Oriental, almost like a sari. But those were comparatively rare occasions.

The most important person to whom I was introduced by Morvarid was of course her thesis supervisor, the formidable Dr Elizabeth Jameson, the Gertrude Bell Professor of English Literature. Morvarid told me her tutor was interested to meet me and was inviting me to have tea with her.

'She was engaged to a Canadian pilot during the War,' Morvarid briefed me about her tutor. 'He was shot down over Dieppe. She never got over her loss. This may account, at least partly, for her eccentricity.'

'I have to wear a skirt,' Morvarid continued in a slightly apologetic tone as we were walking along the tree-shaded streets of North Oxford towards her tutor's home. 'Elizabeth doesn't approve of girls wearing slacks, except for sports. Actually she would prefer me to continue wearing a sari, but that is demanding too much.'

The Gertrude Bell Professor of English Literature lived in a large Victorian-looking house surrounded by a much neglected garden. Unlike Morvarid, I like neglected gardens with their long grass, wild yellow flowers and melancholy atmosphere. I think Wordsworth would have liked Professor Jameson's garden. The old lady lived in her mansion, alone with four or five big dogs. Inside the house looked very dusty, with cobwebs hanging here and there.

'She has a cleaning woman coming about once a month,

but she does a very poor job,' Morvarid explained to me afterwards. 'And the dogs always make a mess.'

I didn't mind the dust and I didn't notice any mess produced by the dogs. I was amazed by the amount of books I saw. I had never seen so many books in a private home. All the walls were lined with bookcases from floor to ceiling. But even they couldn't contain everything and there were books on tables, books on chairs, books on the floor, books on the stairs. Piles of them.

'And do you know?' said Morvarid, 'She has read all of them, from cover to cover. Except the encyclopaedias and dictionaries of course.'

Our hostess turned out to be a frail white-haired lady in a black dress. From her delicate pale-white face I got the impression that she must have been quite a beauty in her youth. She received us in her sitting-room which looked somewhat cleaner than the entrance hall. The walls were likewise lined with bookcases. Heavy Victorian furniture stood on a large genuine Iranian carpet. Over the mantelpiece I saw a faded photograph of a young man in RCAF uniform. We were offered tea in beautiful Chinese cups. Our hostess seemed to have taken it for granted that Morvarid and I were as good as engaged:

'You are a very lucky man, Dr O'Malley. Such a marvellous girl! But what a loss for Oxford! I had been hoping she would stay on at Lady Margaret Hall as a tutor after she gets her D.Phil. But what can we do?'

'Well, Madam,' I answered, 'if you could help me to get a position as a junior lecturer in Persian or a library assistant in the Bodleian I shall be most happy to stay in Oxford with Morvarid.'

'I have no doubt about your scholarship, Dr O'Malley,'

replied the old lady. 'I am sure you would be a great asset to our University, but your discipline is so far from mine, I can do nothing to help you.'

I noticed that Morvarid was calling her tutor by her first name, Elizabeth, not the usual Oxford custom. I expressed my surprise to her as we were walking back.

'And do you think she would make it any easier for me because she considers me a personal friend, sort of adopted daughter?' answered Morvarid. 'No, Sir! She would fail me without the least hesitation if she thought my work was not up to her standard. Last year she had made me rewrite a chapter in my thesis three times before she was satisfied.'

*   *   *

Shortly after New Year I caught a horrible flu. At least I think it was flu. Late in the evening I had escorted Morvarid home by bus, then stood waiting at the bus stop to take the bus back to town. I waited for about 15 minutes, no bus came. I must have missed the last bus. No taxi in sight. I began to walk back towards town. I was shivering. Of course British winter is nothing like our Canadian winter. During my undergraduate days we used to row on the Isis which never froze, whatever the weather. Yet British winter can be quite vicious. It is the dampness which makes it so, a dampness which penetrates right into your bones. By the time I reached my Pembroke Street door I was all drenched by rain mixed with snow flakes. Once inside my room, I took a large gulp of whisky. This will take care of it, I thought. I stripped off my drenched clothes and threw myself on the bed.

I woke up the next morning sneezing and coughing. With great effort I put on a sweater and pants and dragged myself downstairs for breakfast.

'You look ill, Professor O'Malley,' said the landlady. 'Let me give you an aspirin. But you should eat your breakfast first.'

I didn't feel much like having breakfast, the usual stale toast, bacon and eggs, but the strong hot tea revived me a little. I crawled back into my room and again threw myself on the bed. I must have laid there a couple of hours. I don't think I was asleep. I clearly remember watching through the large window the thick grey clouds moving slowly across the sky. Then the telephone rang. It was Morvarid. She was anxious to know whether I had got safely home the evening before.

'Oh yes,' I answered. 'I am all right.'

'Your voice sounds groggy.'

'Oh, just a little cold. I'll be all right tomorrow.'

'You stay where you are! I am coming to investigate. Right now!' she said in an authoritative-sounding tone.

She arrived within half an hour or 45 minutes. I tried to rise to greet her, but my strength failed me and I fell back on my pillows. She touched my forehead.

'You have temperature!' she exclaimed. 'You must stay in bed. Don't you dare to go out in this weather!'

'I have to go out to eat,' I protested. I was beginning to feel hungry, since I had hardly touched Mrs Penny's breakfast. 'Breakfast is included in the rent,' I explained, 'but it isn't enough.'

'I shall take care of that,' answered Morvarid. 'You just sit quiet and do as I tell you. I am not your girlfriend, I am your doctor. I shall be back in about half an hour.'

She returned with two plastic bags in her hands.

'I am going to cook curry for you,' she announced. 'It won't be as elaborate as the one I used to cook at the Curtises, but with the facilities I have here . . . I must borrow a large pot from your landlady.'

I ate the curry with real pleasure, feeling my strength returning.

She also brought several cans of concentrated orange juice. She opened one can, mixed it with water in a glass jar and placed it in the fridge. (Actually she never called it 'fridge'. She always said 'refrigerator'.) She put the unopened cans in the freezer.

'Drink a lot of this,' she instructed me. 'It will make your temperature go down. And vitamin C will strengthen you against further cold. I don't believe in pills from the chemist.'

She came to cook for me every day. In spite of the restricted facilities the curry was always delicious and every time a little different. She told me her dish never tastes the same twice.

Joyce came with her several times. She brought me apologies from her husband who couldn't come because he was 'extremely busy'. I was a little surprised that he should have been so busy during the Christmas holiday, with no work to correct, but no doubt he was very busy with his research. Publish or perish!

I don't know whether I would have survived the two or three weeks of illness without Morvarid. It wasn't so much the cooking (although that was highly appreciated of course), it was the moral support which gave me the will to live and recover.

'When you get ill I shall take care of you,' I said to her as she was preparing to leave one evening.

'I may remind you of it one day,' she answered laughing. 'A Hindu sadhu or holy man had once looked at my hand and told me I shall become very ill some time in my fifties. But,' she added seriously, 'we Parsees don't believe in Hindu superstitions. And I am still not prepared to promise you marriage and the chance to take care of me. So don't take me for granted.'

Her words should have upset me, but they didn't. She stood before me, in a white blouse and narrow black trousers, slowly buttoning a dark blue cardigan before putting on her winter coat. The sight of her in European clothes reassured me not to take her words seriously. Hadn't she changed her apparel as a sign to herself, to me, to the world that she was my girl? Western clothes were more practical for British (or Canadian) winter weather, but the other Indian girls in Oxford wore saris in all weathers, with a heavy winter coat on top if necessary. But Morvarid was different. Of course there was no question of kissing her goodbye with my flu.

During her absence I drank the orange juice as she had instructed me. It was very cold from the fridge, so I added a generous amount of gin to it. 'Doctor' Morvarid Cama didn't exactly approve, but resigned herself to warn me not to put in too much gin.

Father Pereira came to visit me and brought me Communion. I was glad he didn't propose to perform Extreme Unction for me! But he did offer to hear my confession. More out of a desire to talk than from a genuine sense of contrition I agreed. I hadn't gone to confession for years. It has largely gone out of usage after Vatican II although it remains one of the Seven Sacraments. I told him of my guilty feelings about watching Joyce (of course I didn't mention the name), a married woman, and getting a sexual kick out of it.

'Oh, my son! Temptation is not a sin! All of us men experience it,' my confessor calmed me. It seemed clear to me that he included himself among 'all of us men'.

My physical desire for Morvarid? I shouldn't worry about that, since I firmly intended to marry her, but I should pray to

God to grant me patience until that eagerly awaited time arrives.

*　　*　　*

I would have had many more visitors if my illness had occurred during term time. But one of the many strange rules governing student discipline in Oxford has been the rule prohibiting undergraduates who have homes in Britain to reside in Oxford during University holidays. (Of course the rule did not apply to me as a Canadian when I was an undergraduate.) Thus Mrs Penney's rooming house was almost empty except for myself and an American Rhodes Scholar named Bill Clayton. He used to bring me my daily newspaper (usually *The Guardian*) as well as books from the City Library across St Aldate's Street. He had moved into our Pembroke Street rooming house after some scandal involving the maid of his previous landlady. I had heard all sorts of rumours, some sounding plausible, some less so. He loved my Turkish coffee, which, he maintained, counterbalanced the effect of the marijuana cigarettes he used to smoke.

'But I never inhale,' he explained to me half apologetically, 'so I won't get hooked.'

He passionately opposed the war in Vietnam and claimed to be a draft dodger.

'I am not a pacifist,' he explained to me his position, 'and that makes it more difficult for me. American law has come to accept pacifists, Quakers, Jehovah's Witnesses and others who refuse to participate in any war as legitimate conscientious objectors. But, it says, we cannot choose our wars. We can't say we refuse to take part in a particular war because that particular war is immoral. Well, I think the war in Vietnam is immoral. Man, it is criminal! Burning people with napalm! What for? To save them from Communism. As if the fascist oligarchy which has come to rule America is any better. You know what happened at Kent State University? It's only the beginning. Today it is Vietnam, tomorrow I don't know. Maybe it will be the turn of your country.'

'You mean the United States may invade Canada?' I asked.

'If you elect a Communist or Socialist government. I mean real Socialist, not like the British Labour. If you quit NATO and declare non-alignment, if you expel the American military bases, if you nationalize or just overtax the Canadian branches of American multinational corporations, you will get it, man! Granted, this is not likely to happen. More likely it will be Cuba or Libya; or maybe your girlfriend's country. Her government is getting a little too friendly with Russia. Or maybe Iraq. With all those arms they are getting from Russia they are becoming a threat to our ally Israel.'

'But,' he continued, 'I am not an anarchist. I am not one of those guys who burn the American flag, although I understand their frustration. I still believe in America. I was born in a place called Hope, a small town in Arkansas. The name has always inspired me. One day I shall become the President of the United States. I shall restore the true America of Jefferson and Lincoln. I shall never bomb the people of any country with napalm or otherwise. But first of all I shall put an end to the economic blockade of Cuba. Sure, Castro is a Communist dictator. So what? It is criminal to use deprivation of food and medication as a weapon!'

His eyes were flashing and his hands were trembling with anger as he spoke. Oh! the idealism, the enthusiasm and above all the sincerity of youth, whether in love or in politics! If only it could last!

My illness passed and was soon forgotten. No, not really. I couldn't forget the way Morvarid had helped me to get through it. I felt it had created a stronger bond between us than before, notwithstanding her continued refusal to say yes. Our idyll resumed its normal course until a rainy evening during Trinity Term when a loud knock on my door awoke me to the necessity of a quick action.

CHAPTER X

I was sitting in my room typing the notes I had made in the Library. Morvarid had again gone to London with Joyce for a few days. She wasn't sure when exactly she would be coming back. I heard heavy footsteps coming up the stairs. No doubt one of the undergraduate tenants. I paid no attention. Suddenly two loud knocks banged on my door. Why so loud? I remembered the horror stories about visits by Black-and-Tans and SAVAK. 'Come in!' I shouted somewhat irritated. Jack! He had never come to visit me before, neither during my illness nor at any other time.

'Hello, Sean!' he greeted me without smiling. 'We haven't had a talk for a long time.'

'Do come in!' I repeated in a much happier tone. 'Give me your umbrella. Sit down. Let's have a beer.'

'Beer?' Jack twisted his face. 'Don't you have something stronger, man?'

From any other guest I would have found the demand, especially the tone in which it was expressed, rather impertinent, not expected from an Oxford gentleman, but I had been Jack's guest for ten days or two weeks and I had drunk a lot of liquid stronger than beer in his home.

'Are you going to drive home?' I asked apprehensively.

'Of course not!' he answered. 'Joyce has taken the car, as she always does, to go to London. Morvarid has gone with her. Didn't you know?' he asked, sounding a little surprised, probably at my unexpected ignorance of Morvarid's whereabouts.

'I know Morvarid has gone to London with Joyce,' I answered, 'but I didn't know how they had gone. Maybe by bus or train?'

'You can be sure Joyce would take the car whenever she wants,' said Jack with a slight tone of sarcasm in his voice. 'I shall go home by bus or walk if the rain stops, so you don't have to worry about my getting too drunk to drive.'

'OK,' I said, 'I have sherry and Irish whiskey.'

'Sherry is for ladies! Let's have some of your Irish whiskey.'

He took a big gulp. 'We haven't spoken to each other for a long time,' he repeated again. Presumably this statement was meant as a preface to the question that would follow:

'Did you make Morvarid wear European clothes instead of a sari?'

'Goodness no!' I exclaimed in surprise. 'I cannot tell her what to wear, what not to wear!'

'But you encouraged her?' he insisted.

'I don't know what you mean by encouragement' I replied. 'Every woman expects men to compliment her when she puts on a new outfit.'

'But you really like the change in her appearance, don't you?' he continued.

'She sure has good taste,' I answered. 'I had known some Indian girls who looked really beautiful in saris, but very sloppy in European clothes.'

'And you like the look of her in slacks, don't you?' he thrust again.

'She has a good figure,' I answered, trying to sound as insouciant as I could. I was beginning to get annoyed by this inquisitive probe.

'Indeed she has! indeed she has!' said Jack wistfully, as if speaking to himself. 'And you want to have her, all for yourself,' he continued, obviously addressing himself to me. 'Do you think that's fair?'

'What is unfair about wanting to marry a girl I love?' I asked in surprise. 'True, it is against her religion to marry an outsider, but the decision is hers to make.'

'You had met her in my home,' answered Jack. 'I had told you about her and me. I had told you I loved her.'

'If I remember correctly you did tell me you had loved her and had asked her to marry you. She didn't accept and introduced you to Joyce. You fell in love with Joyce and married her. I understand that chapter is closed. Morvarid is free to marry whomever she wants, isn't she?'

'Did I tell you I had fallen in love with Joyce?' asked Jack, sounding slightly surprised. 'It wasn't love, it was sex! Maybe I did delude myself for a short while into thinking it was love. The little bitch! She is marvellous for sex! Also she's a splendid horsewoman. But that's all there is to her.'

I felt mildly disgusted by his words (after all he was talking about his wife), but I was pleased to hear the term 'bitch' being modified by the adjective 'little'. Of course to call a woman a bitch is deeply contemptuous, but the expression 'little bitch' gives the impression of some coquettish charm. It is almost an endearment.

'I think you are being grossly unfair to Joyce,' I said. 'I think she is a very fine woman. Intelligent, Oxford-educated, warm, sensitive, artistic, a charming hostess . . . '

'You like her?' I exclaimed Jack joyfully. 'Great! You can have her after we get divorced. Her marriage to me will be considered invalid by your Church if she becomes a Roman Catholic. It wasn't even an Anglican marriage. We just had a civil marriage. She can marry you in a white dress and veil. Of course, she won't be a virgin, but we are living in the second half of the twentieth century.'

Actually I had often wondered whether she was a virgin when she and Jack had made love during that horseback excursion to Boar's Hill. I suspected not, judging by the readiness with which she had given herself to Jack. But that was irrelevant.

'Very probably I would have been seriously interested in her if she were unmarried and if I hadn't met Morvarid,' I answered quite sincerely. 'But you are married to her. What difference does it make what kind of marriage you had? I know many couples in Canada who are just living together. They didn't have a religious marriage because they don't believe in religion. They had no civil marriage because they think it's a bourgeois convention. Yet their commitment to each other could put to shame many couples married in church or in the registry office. Didn't you make a commitment, a promise when you married Joyce?'

Jack smiled: 'You think I am going to leave Joyce in the lurch? Let me reassure you: I do have my honour. The house will be for her. And all the contents of the house. Except my books of course!' he added in a slightly frightened voice. 'The car is also for her,' he continued, regaining his composure. 'As if she didn't take it whenever she wants anyway. And half of my money in the bank. Don't you think it will make a fair settlement?'

'Materially speaking, probably,' I answered. 'But do you think it's OK to marry a girl and then to try to buy her off with a monetary settlement, however generous, when you get tired of her?'

'Now who's talking?' counterasked Jack with an ironic smile. 'Isn't it how Islamic law (*shari'a* you call it?) in your Iran works? A man can divorce his wife any time if he pays her the sum agreed upon before hand, no? I didn't have such an agreement with Joyce, but I am prepared to give her the house, the car and half of my money. She will be pleased, I assure you! She will be free to marry whomever she wants and I will be free to marry Morvarid. With my don's salary I will be able to support her quite comfortably.'

'And do you think Morvarid will accept to marry you if you divorce Joyce?' I asked with a slight feeling of apprehension. After all she had loved him before she had met me.

'I don't know,' answered Jack quietly with a very sad expression in his eyes. 'To be frank, I don't think I have much chance. Maybe ten percent, maybe one percent. But I don't think all hope is lost. You tell me Morvarid is still undecided about you. That means I still have a chance, however slight. I have made a tragic mistake. I shall do everything in my power to repair it, even if I am to die in the process!' I could sense the intense sincerity in the tone of his voice.

'We all make mistakes in life,' I said, in a clumsy attempt to comfort him with a cliché. 'This is why I find the idea of reincarnation so attractive, although it is against Catholic doctrine.' I made a mental note to discuss it with Father Pereira next time.

'I don't want to marry Morvarid in the next life!' parried Jack angrily. 'I don't know if there is any life other than this one! So we'd better try to correct our mistakes if we can, right now. Let me tell you as it really happened, now that I can see it clearly. Give me more of your Irish whiskey.'

'Of course! I am sorry.' I felt embarrassed I hadn't noticed his glass was empty. He took a large sip.

'I loved Morvarid more than I have loved any woman before or since,' he began. 'Why am I saying "since"? I haven't loved any other woman since I met Morvarid. I told you I didn't really love Joyce. But there was no physical desire in my love for her, I mean Morvarid, not Joyce. She was too pure, too sacred for that. There was a religious sect in sixteenth century Bengal called the Shahajyas. Their leader was the poet Chandi Das. They used to worship the woman they loved, sit her upon an altar and burn incense in front of her. It's OK with Hindu pantheism. Anyone (or anything) can be worshipped as God. While I didn't consider sitting Morvarid upon an altar and burning incense in front of her (I don't think she would have liked that) my sentiments towards her were very much like the poems of Chandi Das. What did I expect when I proposed marriage to her? I expected that, once we were married, in the intimacy of our bedroom sex would show up and take its legitimate place. As I had told you Morvarid did not accept my proposal, although she didn't entirely rule out the possibility. She insisted to introduce me to Joyce. I felt a tremendous sexual desire for Joyce. I told myself: This is something natural, a man's desire for a girl. Sure, sex isn't everything there is to love, but it is the basis upon which all normal love rests. Shahajya love or Western romantic love . . . '

'Or Udhri love in Arabic poetry' I interjected.

'Those are the products of sick minds, I thought. Any psychiatrist will tell you that. Besides, Morvarid will almost certainly refuse me in the end. Why should I run after an impossible ideal? Be realistic, man. So, as a good realist I married Joyce. I decided to give up romantic Orientalism, not academic Orientalism of course, my living depends on it, as does yours. I was pleased when Joyce decided to dye her hair blonde, just to convince myself that I no longer cared for Oriental women and their black hair. Made her even more sexy and enjoyable.'

'Blonde hair is not necessarily incompatible with romantic

Orientalism,' I said. 'Pierre Loti liked his Oriental women blonde. That's why he preferred Turkish women above all others. He flirted with all sorts of girls, Japanese, Tahitian, Senegalese, but the only women he really loved were blonde Turkish women like Aziyade and Djénane. Actually the real model for Djenane was a Frenchwoman pretending to be a Turk, but she deceived Loti quite easily. Too bad for Loti. Good for literature. Have you read *Les Désenchantées*?'

'Yea, Joyce recommended it to me and insisted that I read it.'

'Then we have Yillah, the Polynesian heroine of Melville's *Mardi*,' I continued. 'To make her fit his feminine ideal Melville makes her an albino through some magic process. I won't consider all those blonde Arabian Nights princesses from Hollywood. That's plain vulgarity and ignorance. Anyway, speaking for myself, I don't agree with Loti or Melville. To me black hair is the ideal of femininity and of the Orient.'

'Same here,' answered Jack. 'So, my seeing Joyce dye her hair blonde symbolized my renunciation of Orientalism. And of romantic love. Only sex was real. And yet I was pleased, if a little embarrassed at first, when Joyce invited Morvarid to stay with us and she accepted. I was happy to have her around. I think . . .'

'Oh yes! You were happy to have her around,' I interrupted. 'You treated her like a servant. You had made her your cook.'

Jack's face took an expression of surprised horror. His hands and lips trembled for a few minutes before he spoke:

'Where did you get such an impression? Did Morvarid complain to you or was it from your own observation? You imply that Joyce and I were treating her with some kind of disrespect. If you got such an impression it certainly wasn't intentional on our part. I can speak for Joyce as well as for myself here. Yes, Morvarid did cook for us very often, but we had never asked her to. She had told us cooking was an artistic expression for her. We appreciated it. Anyway, she stopped cooking for us at about the same time as she began wearing European clothes. I don't know if there was any connection between the two. Her personality has changed in so many ways after you came along . . . '

'Of course there was a connection!' I interrupted. 'Her putting on Western clothes was an act of liberation. It was to show you that from now onwards she was a free woman, no longer the little Indian girl, submissive to her English sahib.'

'What the Hell are you accusing me of?' shouted Jack. 'Such an idea never entered my head!'

'No,' I answered calmly, 'but you had taken advantage of her in a way no English girl would have let you. So she began to dress like an English girl to show you she expected to be treated like one.'

'Did she tell you that?'

'No, but I understood it was part of her self-realization. Actually she told me she felt more at ease in Western clothes while going around with a Western man.'

'And I could have been that man,' said Jack grimly, sounding as if speaking to himself. 'But to continue: I was happy enough, at least I thought I was. I had full sexual gratification with Joyce and a beautiful friendship with Morvarid. I didn't consciously realize that I was in love with Morvarid all the time. Until you came along.'

'If you blame me for destroying the peace of your cosy *ménage à trois* why did you invite me in the first place?' I asked. 'You knew I was going to meet her, didn't you?'

'Firstly I didn't know Joyce and I would be held up in Paris by that bloody strike on the day you were supposed to arrive and that you would be spending the night alone under one roof with her,' answered Jack. 'Thank God nobody learned about it, especially none of the Oxford Indians. That had put you in a position of advantage, I suspect. Otherwise, all Oxford admires Morvarid. All of them, all of us,' he corrected himself, 'would throw themselves, ourselves into the river for her as they did for Zuleika Dobson. But you were the first, as far as I am aware, to have gone after her and somehow you have succeeded in winning her favour. Well, you opened my eyes to two things I hadn't been aware of: One: You made her wear European clothes . . .'

'But I didn't!' I interrupted. 'It was her decision.'

'All right,' agreed Jack somewhat grudgingly. 'She decided to wear European clothes when going out with you, as you have just told me. When I first saw her in blouse and slacks instead of a sari I almost fainted! She looked like . . . I don't have to tell you. You know. Why had I run after Joyce instead of sticking to her? I had thought Joyce more sexy. But now I discovered Morvarid had both: Oriental beauty and Western sex appeal. Of the latter even more than Joyce. I realized I had been loving Morvarid, not Joyce all along. Now, with all my inhibitions gone I discovered I loved Morvarid in every way, spiritually (if that's the word for it) and physically. When I was fucking Joyce I fantasized, in the darkness of the night, that I was fulfilling my love for Morvarid. But I couldn't deceive myself for long. There is a couch in our bedroom and now I sleep on that couch, not in Joyce's bed.'

I remembered Morvarid had told me some time earlier that she felt relations had somehow soured or at least cooled down between Jack and Joyce. They hadn't told her anything, but she could feel something was going wrong.

'But that wasn't at all,' continued Jack. 'The second thing

you made me aware of was my lost opportunity. After all a Parsee girl may decide to wear European clothes and still be determined not to marry a non-Parsee. We often get the wrong message from the way a woman dresses. But Morvarid has told Joyce and me that she is seriously considering marrying a non-Parsee, namely you. Instead of you it could have been me if I hadn't allowed myself to get hooked by Joyce. What a stupid blunder I had made!'

'We all make blunders in our relations with women,' I said. 'How many girls had I lost through my tactlessness and stupidity!'

'I take it that had been before you met Morvarid?' said Jack. 'Now, when you had lost a girl you loved didn't you try to repair your mistake and win her back?'

'I sure did!' I answered. 'I had done some really crazy things. Got me nowhere. In retrospect I am pleased.'

'I can see why,' said Jack in a gloomy tone. 'Well, I intend to do my utmost to repair my mistake and win Morvarid back. The first step is of course I must divorce Joyce. After that you can help me.'

'What?' I exclaimed in surprise. 'No way! If you want to divorce Joyce, that is your own business, but I wouldn't help you with Morvarid, even if I could. Just to satisfy my curiosity, please tell me what do you expect me to do?'

'You can step aside.'

'What do you mean?'

'I don't know how many months it is since you proposed to Morvarid. Since she hasn't given you an answer, she is free to tell you "Sorry, no", isn't she? It should apply both ways. A contract isn't binding until both sides have agreed. You can tell her that, since she can't make up her mind for such a long time, maybe you should split.'

115

'Hell, no!' I shouted. I felt like ordering him out of my room, but I just couldn't throw out a guest who had offered me full hospitality, not just a glass of whiskey. Besides, he was Morvarid's landlord and I wanted to avoid a quarrel with him if possible. 'I gave Morvarid my word and I am not going to back out on it. If her mind isn't made up, mine is. True, she isn't committed to me, but I am committed to her. She can keep me waiting all my life. But I hope she won't.'

'I thought you were my friend,' said Jack in a resigned tone, 'but you have turned out to be a dangerous rival.'

'Dangerous rival?' I asked smiling. 'I would take it as a compliment! Do you know, this is what Freud had called Jung, when Jung set up his own school of psychoanalysis involving mysticism, astrology, synchronicity, all those occult concepts Freud was dead against. Yet Freud and Jung had been great friends at one time. Jung had regarded Freud as his guru, to use your terminology. But the break was inevitable. Later, when Hitler invaded Austria, Jung wanted to help Freud, who was a Jew . . . '

'Yes, I know.'

' . . . to find refuge in Switzerland. Freud refused. Fortunately he was able to find refuge in England shortly before he died. So, our rivalry is a reflection of the quarrel of two great men. Morvarid is our psychoanalysis.'

'Well, Dr Jung,' said Jack standing up, 'I'd better be going. It's getting late.'

'Wait a moment! Sit down!' I ordered. 'I have to tell you something.' I am not an authoritarian person, indeed I loathe all manifestations of authoritarianism, but this time I had to make him listen:

'When Morvarid had accepted to become your tenant she was trusting you that you would behave honourably towards her, whatever had gone between you and her in the past. Of course, you were married to Joyce, happily or otherwise. Now you tell me you are divorcing Joyce because of your abiding feelings for Morvarid. I take it that you are an honourable man and will not betray her trust by going after her in a way which she may find abusive. You know the East and the sensitivities of Oriental women.'

'I don't know what exactly you mean by me going after her in an abusive way,' answered Jack. 'If you fear I may try to approach her physically, let me assure you. I am an Oxford man. In Oxford we are taught to be gentlemen first and academics afterwards. Not everyone takes that seriously, but I do. But I don't see what's dishonourable about telling a woman I had once loved that I still love her. True, I am legally married to someone else now, but I am getting divorced. People do get divorced and remarried. Morvarid is currently dating another man, but, as far as I know, she isn't engaged to him yet. Oxford girls date all sorts of men before they get married. So I see no reason why I shouldn't speak to her about it.'

'Go ahead,' I said with resignation. 'But you are still her landlord. Don't you think that making a declaration of love, with or without a marriage proposal, while she is living in your home will put her in an unfairly awkward situation? You would be like a tutor making a declaration of love to a student. How can she continue staying in your home after that?'

'I won't remain her landlord for long,' answered Jack grimly. 'I told you I am going to leave the house to Joyce. I'd better move out immediately. I can't continue living with a woman with whom I am getting divorced. As an unmarried don I shall be entitled to a room in the College. The privilege should apply to a don about to be divorced. I'll enquire tomorrow.

Hope they have a spare room. But it will take a couple of days to move my books, my clothes. What a mess! I'd better be going. Good night, Dr Jung.'

'Good night, Dr Freud.'

We shook hands, a long, firm handshake. I thought we were like two boxers shaking hands before their fight. Professional boxers often hate each other's guts, but gentlemen boxers may be good friends before and after their fight. At least their courtesy towards each other has to be impeccable. This is the British idea of gentlemen's sportsmanship as professed in Oxford (and in the Other Place). I am not a boxer (I wouldn't count the street fights I had engaged in as a kid) so I'd better think of a different, more personal occasion of shaking hands with an adversary: Some years earlier I had been summoned by the Principal of McGill to be disciplined for my participation in a student protest against his attempt to censor their newspaper, *The McGill Daily*. (I am a firm believer in unlimited free speech.) The old gentleman, as old-fashioned in his conservative authoritarian ideas as in his exquisitely courteous manners (more British than Canadian) began the mini-trial by solemnly shaking hands with me. Faced with the threat of dismissal I was naturally apprehensive although I felt I had done nothing wrong. I was feeling just as apprehensive now.

CHAPTER XI

The visit had left me in a turmoil. In many ways I could see myself in Jack. The conflict between ideal and sensual love, and the discovery that Morvarid could be the source of inspiration for both . . . I too could have married a sexy Joyce and then found myself confronted by my feminine ideal. But more urgent matter: I was afraid for Morvarid when she would return to his home. She had told me she didn't know how long she was going to stay in London. Hopefully she was going to stay long enough for Jack to move all his things out. While I trusted Jack's honour as an Oxford gentleman not to make any crude advances towards her, a declaration of love by her married landlord, however courteously expressed, would surely send her into a panic. Also, there was Jack sober and Jack drunk who might not be in full control of his words (if he would be in full control of his actions). I remembered his words to me: 'When I was fucking Joyce I fantasized, in the darkness of the night, that I was fulfilling my love for Morvarid.' I noticed the difference in the vocabulary, but nevertheless I felt the man was dangerous. I must warn Morvarid immediately!

Just then I heard Great Tom strike eleven. Too late to phone Joyce's aunt with whom the two women stayed whenever they went to London. First thing in the morning, I decided. I spent a sleepless night thinking what would be the earliest suitable time for 'first thing in the morning'. I had never phoned Joyce's aunt before. Could I call her at eight? Certainly too early. Eight thirty? Nine? I gathered my courage at nine thirty.

'Hello?' an elderly woman's voice answered.

'Good morning, Madam. I hope I am not too early calling. May I speak to Miss Cama, please?'

'Is it Professor O'Malley?' asked the voice. Evidently Morvarid and Joyce had told her about me. 'I am sorry, Sir. The girls have just left.'

'Sorry to disturb you, Madam,' I said. 'I shall call again in the evening.'

'Joyce will be back in the evening. She is staying with me two more nights,' said the aunt, 'but Morvarid is going back to Oxford tonight. She won't be coming back here.'

I was flabbergasted. She is coming back alone, without Joyce, to face Jack! God knows what he will tell her and how he will say it if he happens to be drunk. She had told me her landlord had been drinking heavily lately. She thought he was worried about something. I could guess what it was. Since his visit last night I knew for sure. I must meet her when she gets off the train or the coach to warn her. Train or coach? A good question.

'Do you know whether she will be going by coach or train?' I asked Joyce's aunt.

'I am afraid I cannot tell you, Sir. The girls were talking about it at breakfast. Morvarid said something about the coaches being more frequent than the trains.'

She would probably take the coach. But not necessarily. Should I wait for her at the coach terminal or the train station? Anyway, she wouldn't be coming till late in the afternoon at the earliest. I spent the morning in the Bodleian trying to take my mind off my worry. After lunch in the coach station cafeteria I began to walk between the coach and train station, coach and train schedules in my hand. It is the poorer, 'slummy' part of Oxford, vividly described by Thomas Hardy in *Jude the Obscure*. University people seldom ventured there except when going to and from the train station. I had also found the district dismal, but I loved the Oxford Canal, although not as strongly as a kindred spirit, my fellow-Orientalist James Elroy Flecker, who had declared:

'It is dearer to me than the antique town.'

Now I crossed that canal several times without stopping on Hythe Bridge to contemplate it as I had done in the past. I saw people getting off the London coaches and trains, but no sign of Morvarid. I must have missed some coaches and some trains. Later it occurred to me that, not knowing how she would be coming, I could have stood in front of the Curtises' house, her final destination and waited for her there, perhaps hiding behind a tree from Jack's view. But then what could I have told her seeing her alight from a bus or taxi? 'Don't go in because Jack may be dangerous'? That would have really scared her! Meeting her at the coach or train station and inviting her to a cafe, where I could leisurely explain the situation to her was a different matter. But it was not to be.

I returned to my room and dialled the Curtises' number. 'Yes!?' I heard Jack's angry voice. Not his usual composed, 'Curtis speaking'. I called Joyce's aunt again. Fortunately Joyce was back from town. Of course I made no mention of what Jack had told me the previous evening. I merely asked: 'How did you send Morvarid back to Oxford? by coach or by train?'

'She wanted me to take her to Victoria Coach Station when we ran into Professor Miles in the British Museum. He was going back to Oxford this afternoon and offered her a lift in his car. She should be home by now. Why don't you call her?'

That explained why I couldn't catch her either at the coach terminal or the train station. But what should I do now? Jack's angry 'Yes!?' only increased my forebodings. Suddenly my telephone rang. Morvarid's voice!

'Sean? I am in serious trouble. I can't explain it on the telephone. Can you come?'

'I am coming right now!' I shouted dropping the receiver. I ran out without putting on my raincoat although a small drizzle had started to fall. I ran up Pembroke Street towards St. Aldate's hoping to catch a taxi there. Shit! No taxi in sight. I began to walk along St Aldate's towards Carfax, but it wasn't until I reached Carfax Crossroads that I found a taxi. Within ten or fifteen minutes I was at the Curtises' door. I rang the bell. I was pleased to see Morvarid, not Jack opening the door for me. Morvarid looked very nervous. Her hands and lips were trembling. 'Come up to my room,' she told me, speaking very quickly. 'We can talk better there.'

I followed her. On the way I noticed the door of Jack's study opening slightly and Jack's face watching me with a sulky expression.

I had never been inside Morvarid's bedroom. She had always received me in the Curtises' sitting-room. Now, in spite of the urgency of the situation I took in the room at a glance. It looked very much like a typical Oxford student's room. A large bookcase of course. A desk with a typewriter and some papers on it. A small radio and a record player. One of the legitimate excuses boys and girls could use to invite each other to their rooms in Oxford was to listen to records. More often it was the girls who played the hostesses, collecting records being more of a feminine hobby. Morvarid, knowing my love of Oriental music, had often invited me to listen to her Indian records, but she used to play them in the sitting-room on the Curtises' bigger (and probably better) Japanese stereo. On the wall a portrait of the Prophet Zarathushtra, black-bearded, in a white robe and turban, with rays of light emanating from his head, such as I had seen in Zoroastrian homes in Yazd and Kerman. Some picture postcards showing the Taj Mahal, the Qutb Minar and other architectural monuments of India glued to the opposite wall. But to me the most interesting piece of decor in the room was a framed graduation photo of Morvarid in a black gown with the crimson MA hood draped round her shoulders, a woman's soft mortarboard crowning her head. Yet the neat order of the room was disturbed: The door of the clothes cabinet was wide open. On the bed stood an open suitcase half filled with clothing. Some bits of clothing were on the bed, scattered around the suitcase. I assumed she hadn't finished unpacking since she returned from London. But I was surprised to see in the suitcase, on top of the clothing, the thick Manila folder which I immediately recognized as enclosing the finished chapters of her thesis which I had read with great interest and very welcome comments. No doubt she had taken her thesis to London with her to show it to some professor there.

Morvarid shut the door behind us and turned the key. I remembered my first evening in that house when she had turned that key on me. I had reminded her of it at one time. She remembered:

'I wasn't afraid of you,' she said laughing. 'I could see you were a gentleman. But I had to keep up appearances!'

And now the key was turned with me inside the room, to keep someone else out.

As soon as she had locked the door, Morvarid threw her arms round my neck and began to cry, burying her face against my chest. I felt amazed at the inner fragility of this outwardly

Westernized, trousered Oriental girl. I pressed her to my bosom and stroked her short hair.

'Has Jack been abusive to you?' I asked her, believing I knew the cause of her distress.

'No, I cannot say that,' she answered, regaining her composure. 'He was very polite about it, but what he has told me . . . I am terrified!'

I could guess what it was, but I held my peace in order to let her tell me about it in her own words:

'He told me he no longer loves Joyce, or rather, that he had never loved her. He wants to divorce her. He tells me that he loves me and wants to marry me. The way he put it, he must marry me. I saw such a lustful look in his eyes as he was looking at me. It terrified me! I had noticed such a look in his eyes once before, when he first saw me in European clothes, in slacks, after I had discarded the sari. I didn't pay much attention to it then. I thought it was just the novelty. But now . . . Oh Sean! How right you have been to advise me to leave this house! But I was comfortable and reluctant to move. And now I must leave in a hurry.' She pointed to the open suitcase. 'I cannot stay here with him! No, not a single night!'

I understood the meaning of the various articles of clothing scattered in disorder around her suitcase. She wasn't unpacking from her London trip, she was hurriedly packing to escape somewhere. Packing is harder than unpacking even under normal circumstances. You have to decide what to take, what not to take. And packing in a hurry . . . That also explained the presence of her thesis in the suitcase. She wasn't going to leave that behind in this house!

'Yes, I know,' I said. 'He came to see me last night and told me he intended to divorce Joyce and propose marriage to you. I expected it would be a shock for you to hear it from him, so I wanted to warn you beforehand. It was too late to phone Joyce's aunt, after eleven, so I called in the morning. She told me you and Joyce had already left for town and that you would be returning to Oxford by yourself today. I didn't know whether you would be coming by coach or train so I spent the afternoon walking from coach station to train station back and forth . . . '

'Poor you!' exclaimed Morvarid. 'I was given a lift by Professor Miles who kindly brought me right to the door.'

'I know,' I said. 'I returned to my room and called Joyce's aunt again. Joyce was back and she told me. Of course I told her nothing of what her husband had told me last night. A few minutes later your phone came, so here I am, all for you. I very well understand you don't want to spend the night here, alone with Jack, with his wife (theoretically she is still his wife) absent. But he has told me he is going to move out as soon as he can. He doesn't want to stay with the woman whom he is about to divorce. He is going to leave the house for Joyce anyway when he divorces her. But I see that tonight he is still here. Do you have a place to go to? I suppose that would be just for a few nights until he moves out, hopefully fast enough.'

'Yes, he has told me the same thing,' said Morvarid. 'He said he has asked Jesus College to give him a room. They will give him one, but not immediately. They are having a conference about Welsh Studies there and all spare rooms are occupied by visiting scholars.' (I remembered reading about that conference in the *Oxford Mail*.) 'They will give him the room once the conference is over. But meanwhile I don't want to be stuck with him here!'

'Do you have a place to go?' I asked again. 'Too bad I don't have a car. We'll have to take a taxi.'

'I have thought of calling LMH,' said Morvarid, 'but I can't descend on them all of a sudden, demanding lodging for the night. Oh yes, the Principal will take me if I explain to her my predicament. But what shall I tell her? That my married landlord has been making romantic advances towards me in the absence of his wife? No, I don't want to make accusations against Jack, even if he deserves it. I hate scandals! I think I shall call Elizabeth and ask her to let me stay in her house for a few nights. She is a real friend and I can tell her everything. Only her house is so dirty...' Morvarid twisted her mouth. 'But the only alternative would be to go to a hotel. Anyway, let me finish packing my suitcase. Then we shall go down to the telephone and I shall call Elizabeth.'

She was obviously reluctant to make that phone call, perhaps because she knew that Jack would be listening. Her packing was a (perhaps subconscious) delaying tactic. Anyway, with my reassuring presence, she finished her packing quickly enough. We went down to the sitting-room. Again I saw the door of Jack's study open slightly with Jack's face staring at us. I don't know whether Morvarid had noticed him. She lifted the receiver and dialled the number:

'Elizabeth? It is I, Morvarid.' (She always used the donnish 'It is I' instead of the common 'It is me'.) 'I am in a predicament. I have big trouble with my landlord. Can't explain it to you on the phone. Could I come and stay in your home for a couple of nights until the matter is solved?...... No, please don't prepare any bed for me. I can sleep on a couch anywhere...... Oh, thank you! thank you! thank you! You are like a mother to me in this country. I shall be coming within half an hour or 45 minutes...'

Just as she hung up the receiver the door of Jack's study opened widely and her landlord burst into the room.

'No, Morvarid!' he exclaimed. 'You are not going to leave now!'

I was amazed at what I thought was his impudence: 'Come on, Jack!' I shouted. 'Be reasonable! She isn't your slave! She's a free woman and can come and go as she wants.'

'You keep out of it, Sean!' he glared at me savagely,' and let me finish. Morvarid! I may have offended you the way I spoke to you an hour or so ago. If so, I beg your forgiveness. Believe me, you are the last person in the world I would want to offend. I may be tactless, but I am not without honour. If you cannot stay with me under one roof, I should be the one to leave. Give me about half an hour to pick up a few things and I'll be off. Hope you don't mind if I come back during the day. All my things, all my books are here. I shall pick up everything and move out for good when that conference at Jesus is over.'

Morvarid looked embarrassed: 'But this is your own home, Jack. I don't want to be the cause of . . . '

'Not any more,' answered Jack. 'It is Joyce's home, as I told you. Joyce is your landlady now. But she cannot throw you out. You have paid your rent till the end of the term. Now excuse me. The sooner I start packing the sooner I'll go.'

He disappeared upstairs. Morvarid and I sat in silence. He came down about ten minutes later with a large travelling bag over his shoulder. Without saying a word to us he went into his study. He stayed there what seemed to me much longer than ten minutes.

'He's probably picking up some books or papers,' I whispered to Morvarid.

Eventually he emerged, his bag looking much more bulky.

'All right, folks,' he said. 'I am going. I have to call a taxi because Joyce has the bloody car. Have an enjoyable evening, the two of you. There's a bottle of champagne in the fridge in the kitchen.'

I thought I could detect a very thin note of sarcasm, of insinuation in the reference to the bottle of champagne. I decided to ignore it, and so I think did Morvarid.

'Where are you going to stay?' I asked him.

'Don't worry about me,' he answered, the polite British way of saying 'Mind your own business'.

The taxi came. Jack extended his hand to Morvarid: 'I hope we are parting as friends. Forgive any tactlessness on my part.' He kissed her hand. Then he extended his hand to me:

'All right, Sean. You seem to be winning this battle. Well, I may be down, but I am not out yet!'

He left.

'I wonder where he will go,' said Morvarid.

'Probably he'll stay with some friends for a few days until he can move into the College,' I said.

'Will he drop on them just like that? We didn't hear him making any phone calls. I am worried about him,' said Morvarid with a tone of anxiety in her voice.

'Oh, he will know how to take care of himself,' I answered impatiently. 'Well, I'd better be going too. You must be real tired after this ordeal. Will you feel safe here now?'

'Oh yes. I have slept here alone many times.'

'I mean safe from him. Suppose he discovers he has forgotten his toothbrush, or, more likely, some book or paper he needs urgently. Of course he has the key...'

'There's a safety chain on the entrance door, haven't you noticed?' answered Morvarid. 'I shall put it on and will not open for Jack or anyone during the night. In the morning it will be different. I don't think I'll be afraid of him during the day.'

128

'All right, but try to keep out of his way. Also, don't wear slacks when he's around. It turns him on,' I said.

'I know,' she whispered.

'It turns me on too,' I said to myself, but audibly enough for her to hear. 'Better wear a sari.'

'No, I will not wear a sari!' answered Morvarid, her eyes flashing vehemently. 'I shall wear a skirt. But I will probably be in the Bodleian when he comes here.'

'Good. So, I'll get going.'

Morvarid stopped me: 'Have you eaten?' she asked me.

'Yes, I had lunch in the coach station cafeteria,' I answered.

'That must have been hours ago! You must be starving! Come, let me prepare an Indian high tea for you. But first I must call Elizabeth and tell her not to expect me. She will think I am crazy. Maybe she won't be very wrong.'

After she made the phone call and explained to her tutor and foster mother that the problem was (at least temporarily) solved I followed her to the kitchen. Out of curiosity I opened the fridge. Indeed there was a bottle of champagne standing there. We did not touch it.

CHAPTER XII

Jack did not come to bother Morvarid the following day nor the next. He just did not show up. Of course he could have come and picked up some of his things while she was out. She didn't notice anything missing nor any telltale sign of Jack (or anybody else) having entered the house during her absence. Jack was a heavy smoker but the ashtray in his study was as clean as she had left it after she had cleaned it the morning after his departure. Trying to avoid facing Jack alone in the house she had spent most of those two days in the Bodleian. In the evening we dined in the Taj Mahal and I walked her home. She was wearing a skirt, as she had said she would. Just in case.

On the second evening we saw the Curtises' black Toyota parked in front of the house. Joyce was back. Morvarid had been both looking forward to and apprehensive about her landlady's return. Looking forward to because she would no longer have to face Jack alone, should he show up in the house. Apprehensive because she would have to explain to her Jack's disappearance and her own, however involuntary, role in it. Like a good Zoroastrian she decided to tell her the whole truth. How would Joyce take it? Would she blame her for the breakdown of her marriage?

Morvarid's fears proved unfounded. I saw her on the following day. She was again wearing trousers, presumably no longer afraid of provoking Jack.

'Joyce took it quite well,' she was telling me, sipping a cup of Darjeeling tea in my Pembroke Street room. 'She was even pleased. "Good riddance," she said. She told me her marriage had been foundering for months and she was very unhappy in it. I could feel something was wrong. She will not oppose the divorce. So they will have a divorce by mutual consent. Shouldn't take long. She told me I can have Jack after they get divorced. I screamed at her and told her I had no designs on him and she apologized. She was very pleased when I said Jack had told me he will leave the house for her. She will not only allow me to stay, but insists I should stay with her until I either get married or leave Oxford. She says I remain her best friend. I feel sorry for both of them. I feel somewhat guilty too. I shouldn't have accepted to become their tenant after what had gone between Jack and me.'

'OK,' I said, 'you had made a mistake, but it was an honest mistake and you shouldn't feel guilty about it. You had no intention to seduce Jack or to mess up their marriage.'

'Oh no!' answered Morvarid, sounding horrified at the idea. 'But . . . the provocative way I began to dress after I had discarded the sari . . . '

'You mean by wearing trousers?' I asked, looking at her trousered legs. 'You have been dressing like most, if not all, Oxford girls. How about his wife? I don't remember ever seeing her in a dress or skirt.'

'She has one black skirt which she puts on whenever she has to wear her gown,' said Morvarid laughing. 'She has told me she had always hated wearing a skirt or dress. But, speaking for myself,' (her voice again became serious) 'deep inside me I knew I was exciting him by what I wore and I felt good about it. I shouldn't have been so coquettish.'

'Come on girl!' I answered. 'Every normal woman has something of a coquette about her and wants to impress men by whatever she is wearing. Otherwise there is something morbidly wrong with her. You're a normal, charming girl, that's all.'

'Really? Do you think so?' asked Morvarid anxiously.

'Really,' I answered. She had finished her tea and put the empty cup aside. I put my arm round her shoulder and kissed her on the nape of the neck.

CHAPTER XIII

Mrs Curtis may not have been displeased by her unloving and unloved husband deserting and intending to divorce her, but she would have liked to know his whereabouts. If they were to get divorced let them start the proceedings, the sooner the better. Presumably one of these days she would be receiving a letter from his lawyer, but meanwhile she was finding herself in a most awkward situation, neither wife nor divorcee.

It all dawned upon her when she received a telephone call from the Oriental Institute enquiring about her husband. Dr Curtis had failed to appear at either of the two courses he was teaching this year: elementary Sanskrit class and the advanced course involving a reading of the Ramayana with a grammatical analysis using Panini's method. Was he ill? A most embarrassing situation. What was she to answer? 'The bum has abandoned me and I don't know where he is'? I don't know if this is what she had actually told them. I did not see her during those days and all my information about the above facts had come to me from Morvarid who had become very much her landlady's confidante.

Enquiries at Jesus College did not help. The Conference on Welsh Studies was over, a room was ready for Dr Curtis's use, but the expected occupant did not show up. Joyce felt compelled to inform the police, not because she was worried about her husband's safety, but because she wanted the messy situation clarified. Thames Valley Police took her call rather nonchalantly, she felt. All dons are, by definition, eccentric (some of them are downright crazy) and one of the many eccentric things they do is to disappear for a few days or even a few weeks without informing their family or college. She was told not to worry, they will find her husband eventually.

Shortly afterwards I received an alarming telephone call from Morvarid: 'Sean! do you know? Jack is in Radcliffe Infirmary in a coma!' He had been found unconscious the day before, not by the cops but by a chambermaid in his room in the Hideaway Hotel where apparently he had been staying since his disappearance. The Hideaway was a cheap, dingy hotel near the train station, a gathering place of prostitutes and drug dealers. Bill Clayton used to go there to buy his marijuana cigarettes. Apparently Jack's coma had been caused by a fatal mixture of alcohol and drugs. I remembered seeing the headline in the *Oxford Mail* the evening before:

DON FOUND IN HIDEAWAY HOTEL IN A COMA

Somehow it didn't occur to me that it might have referred to Jack, and I didn't bother to buy the paper.

Fortunately Jack's coma did not last long and he woke up a day or two later. (I don't know what kind of treatment he had been given: I am very ignorant about medical matters.) Soon afterwards he was allowed visitors. I went with great hesitation. How pleased would he be to receive a visit from his 'dangerous rival'? I had no doubt that his over-indulgence in drugs and booze had been due to his despair over the loss of Morvarid. To my surprise he received me quite cordially:

'Hello, Sean! Got myself into a big mess, haven't I? My doctor, his name is Solomon, is accusing me of having attempted suicide. That's bullshit! I did not have the intention to kill myself. I just didn't care a shit whether I lived or died.

And I still don't. So I have told him. "Oh, but you have a
subconscious death wish" he tells me "and we must cure you
of that". He is neither an Oxford nor Cambridge man. Has his
MD from the University of Manchester.' (Jack twisted his
mouth contemptuously.) 'Afterwards he studied neurology and
psychiatry in the United States. Calls himself a neuro-
psychiatrist. What a mouthful! I just call him a shrink. Divides
his time between this place and Warneford Hospital. Wants to
transfer me to the Warneford after I completely recover from
the dope of the Hideaway. I think I'll go along. What do I care?
I won't be the first nor the last Oxford don in the Warneford.
Let's change the subject. Do you know who came to see me
yesterday? Morvarid! She was wearing a sari. She looked
absolutely beautiful! I hadn't seen her in a sari for months. She
seemed to me like an apparition of ethereal beauty. Again I
told her I loved her. She told me she was most distressed at
having been the unwilling cause of my present condition but
she just couldn't respond to my love. She urged me to get
reconciled with Joyce. I told her no way. I asked her whether
she was going to marry you. She answered she hadn't
promised you anything. Same thing she has been saying all
along during these months. Guess I should wish you good
luck,' he added on a sarcastic note.

I thought it was very considerate on Morvarid's part to have
overcome her aversion against her national dress and put on a
sari when she went to visit Jack in hospital, since the sight of
her in Western clothes used to excite him physically. Why
upset him unnecessarily? To think of it: I had not seen her in a
sari myself for months. Too bad she hadn't called to tell me
she was going to visit Jack. We would have gone together. But
no. She was wise. The sight of the two of us together would
only have hurt Jack. Anyway, I hadn't seen her at all, in a sari

or otherwise, for the past two or three days. She was very busy at that time, putting the final touches to her (almost) finished thesis. I must call her!

'Hello, Sean! You want to see me? Would you like to come for tea tomorrow afternoon? At four o'clock. See you tomorrow. Goodbye!' She hung up.

She sounded rather cold about her invitation, not her usual manner. No doubt she was very tired, tired by finishing her thesis to present it before the deadline, and, most of all, tired by the ordeal of Jack's illness for which she was feeling indirectly responsible.

CHAPTER XIV

On the following day, punctually at four, I was ringing the now familiar bell. Morvarid opened the door. She was wearing an orange sari over a black blouse. Sure, I have my Irishman's bias against the colour orange, but I wasn't so narrow-minded as to expect it to have the same significance all over the world it has in Ireland! In India it is the hallowed symbol of the Hindu religion. To Morvarid, a Zoroastrian, it would have no religious significance. but it would represent a culture with which she identified. Even a Catholic Indian girl may wear an orange sari, innocently unaware of the dismay that colour evokes among her co-religionists in a faraway country. The sari in which Morvarid received me that afternoon was a plain orange sari without a border. I didn't remember ever seeing her wearing that particular sari.

'You are wearing a sari!' I exclaimed in surprise.

'Don't you like it?' she asked me, her voice sounding defiant, her eyes staring at me in an unflinching gaze. I noticed her unsmiling lips wore no lipstick. 'I had heard you so many times bemoan the fact that I had given up the sari. Well, you are seeing me in a sari now.'

'You look lovely!' I exclaimed in all sincerity, putting my arm round her waist and kissing her cheek. 'I was just surprised: You had told me you would never wear a sari again.'

'So I thought at the time,' answered Morvarid sadly. 'I was mistaken. I was like an actress playing a role, the role of a Westernized Oriental woman, the girlfriend, almost the fiancée of a Western man. I was a good actress. I really lived my role! But when the play is over the actress takes off her stage costume and becomes her real self again. From now onwards I shall always wear a sari. I am an Indian, and proud of it. You'd better realize that!' she added, her voice again defiant, her eyes flashing.

OK, I thought, she is proud she is an Indian and wants to show it by wearing a sari. But why is she being so aggressive in telling me about it as if she expected hostility on my part?

'Morvarid!' I exclaimed. 'I shall be just as proud to have you as my wife. I want to take you, wearing your most beautiful sari to the balcony of Montreal City Hall, that same balcony from which de Gaulle had shouted *"Vive le Québec libre!'* and to proclaim: "Look! This beautiful Indian woman is my wife!" With TV cameras turning.'

'Oh Sean!' answered Morvarid, sounding more sad than angry, 'you don't understand! Indian girls, traditional Indian girls that is, don't marry foreigners. Or rather, to be more exact, they don't marry outside their religion. I cannot marry a Hindu, a Muslim, a Sikh or an Indian Christian. Or a foreign Christian,' she added after a pause.

I felt a cold shiver, running down my spine. I remembered Blasco Ibáñez's novella, *Luna Benamor* in which the Jewish heroine tells her Catholic suitor: *'Tu raza no es mi raza, tu Dios no es mi Dios.'* Like the Zoroastrians, the Jews prohibit inter-marriage, but, unlike the Zoroastrians, they accept converts, albeit reluctantly. I had sometimes wondered: If Morvarid were Jewish (there are Indian Jews) would I have agreed to convert to Judaism? No. If she were a Muslim I might have accepted Islam, but a conversion to Judaism would, for a Christian, entail a renunciation of Christ, which a conversion to Islam would not. I guess there are certain principles which take precedence over love, however pure and noble. If we don't believe in those principles ourselves we must respect them when others do.

'I told you I had no right to ask you to act against the principles of your religion, and I must accept the consequences,' I said to Morvarid. 'You have given me the greatest happiness I have had in my life. I knew I may have to pay a very high price for it. I guess the day of reckoning has come.'

'I have done you a great wrong raising your hopes throughout all these months,' answered Morvarid. 'I should have told you no, impossible, right in the beginning. Likewise I should have said a definite no to Jack instead of testing the strength of his love for me by introducing him to Joyce. This is what happens when a Parsee girl starts flirting with boys not of her religion or community: a tragedy.'

'I am very sorry for Jack,' I said, 'but his tragedy is of his own making. He chose to marry Joyce and now he is running away from the consequences. By the way, is Joyce out?' I asked. I didn't want her to overhear our conversation.

'Yes, she is gone to the Bodleian,' answered Morvarid.

'As I have said,' I continued, 'if you cannot marry me because of your religion I respect that, but if it is because you feel guilty about what has happened to Jack I can't accept it. If Jack has messed up his own life and Joyce's, must we mess up ours also? Two wrongs won't make a right. If one man is suffering because he didn't have enough determination in his love for you when he had his chance, must another man suffer also? Will it somehow lessen the iniquity if two men suffer instead of one?'

'Sean, you still don't understand!' answered Morvarid. 'You claim to respect the laws of my religion, but you dismiss my guilt over what has happened to Jack as if they were two different matters. But you can't separate the two! Jack's tragedy is the direct result of my disregard of the principles of my religion. I should never have considered marrying him or you or any non-Parsee.'

'I think I understand,' I said in a dejected voice (at least I thought I sounded most dejected). 'Shall I see you again?'

'If you like,' answered Morvarid. 'I mean, I shall be glad to see you. But not very soon. Give me a couple of weeks to finish my thesis. Of course, I shall be wearing a sari,' she added.

'What will you do when you get your D.Phil.?' I asked her. 'I was hoping to take you to Canada with me. Will you go back to India?'

'I don't think so,' she answered. 'You know Elizabeth has been telling me she wants to get me a fellowship in LMH with a permanent position as a tutor. I had not taken her seriously, but now I see she is really serious. And she is more powerful than the Principal. So hopefully I shall stay in Oxford. I don't want to go back to Bombay if I can help it. Have been away too long to fit into my family's little world. They will want to find a Parsee husband for me, a wealthy businessman most likely.' (She twisted her mouth.) 'They cannot force me, but they can get me sick and tired with their importunities.'

'But you have just said you want to marry a Parsee boy!' I said in surprise.

'I have said nothing of the sort!' answered Morvarid almost angrily. 'I have said I cannot marry a non-Parsee, but I don't have to marry a Parsee or anyone else if I don't want to. I don't think I will ever get married.'

I felt a certain sense of relief. I cannot marry her, but no other man will! My male pride was gratified. Had she been a

Buddhist she probably would have told me she would become a nun. During my third year as an undergraduate in Oxford I had a Japanese girlfriend. She had admitted she loved me, but said she could not marry me because I wasn't Japanese. But she would marry no one else. Upon her return to Japan she would shave her head (she had long black hair) and become a Buddhist nun. She thought it was a most romantic way to end our beautiful but in her view impossible relationship. She promised to send me a photo of herself with her head shaven as a farewell gift to me. With a morbid curiosity I awaited that photo, but it never came. Nor any communication from her. Eventually I gave up on her.

Fortunately or unfortunately there is no nunnery in the Zoroastrian religion. Morvarid would live on in Oxford, a charming, unmarried lady don, most elegant in her saris. The dons would talk about her over glasses of sherry: What a pity that such a beautiful woman has never got married. Was I being selfish in wanting to condemn her to permanent spinsterhood? Not really. There was more than my male instinct of jealousy involved. There was a flicker of hope: as long as she is not married to someone else there is always the possibility, however remote that she may change her mind. And to that particle of hope I was determined to hold on with all my strength.

'I wish I could stay in Oxford, or anywhere in England to be near you,' I said, 'but I'll have to go back to Montreal when my sabbatical year is over.'

'I am both glad and sorry you are going back,' answered Morvarid, her voice expressing the sorrow more than the gladness. 'If you were to stay in Oxford I would find it extremely difficult to continue a steady friendship with a man whom I cannot marry.'

'May I write to you?' I asked her.

'Please do!' she answered. 'I promise I will always reply.'

'I am a member of BRISMES (The British Society for Middle East Studies),' I said. 'They have their Annual Meeting every summer. That would provide as good an excuse as any to come to England. Could I see you then?'

'Yes,' she answered with a slight hesitation. 'I shall be glad to see you. And I will be pleased to meet your wife if she accompanies you on your visit to England.'

'My wife!? What are you talking about!?' I exclaimed in shocked surprise. 'You know I am not married!'

'Not now,' she answered very calmly, 'but you are going to get married one day, aren't you?'

'Hell, no!' I shouted in a fury. 'If you are not going to get married, I am not either. If you cannot marry a non-Parsee I will not marry any woman but you. I will either marry you or no one else!'

I thought I saw a faint smile, as if of pleasure, cross her lips, but maybe it was wishful thinking.

'All right, Sean, I shall see you by yourself. One date per year will not lead us astray from the path of rectitude. I shall be wearing my most glamorous sari. And I will grow my hair long again. Long hair goes better with a sari.' She smiled coquettishly. 'But anyway,' she continued after a pause, 'it is too early to talk about that. I promise to call you when I finish my thesis. It will take me two or three weeks. Then we can discuss our futures.' (I noticed the plural form she used: futures, not future.) 'Now, let me give you some tea.'

Unlike my previous visits to her I didn't feel much like drinking tea, not even her spicy Indian tea which I loved. But I wanted to prolong what I feared might be my last visit. I remembered the lines of Hafez:

Mara dar manzel-e janan che ja-ye 'aysh chu har dam
Jaras avaz mizanad ke bar bandid mahmelha.

(In the home of our beloved what room for joy is there for us
when every moment
The camel bell calls: Pack up your belongings).

CHAPTER XV

So this was her definite answer: She would not marry me and our two futures would run their separate courses. The sky did not fall down. Great Tom beat the hours with his usual regularity. I continued with my work. Indeed, I engrossed myself in my work to keep my mind occupied. In the evenings I drank heavily but never got drunk. My state would have been infinitely worse if Morvarid had decided to cut all communication and refused to see me again. But she had promised to call me when she had finished her thesis. I didn't expect much to come out of that meeting. We would say goodbye (maybe she would allow me to kiss her for the last time) and I would go back to Montreal without her. Yet my future did not look entirely bleak. I would write her long letters. She had promised to reply. Those letters would form the central reality of my life in Montreal. And I would see her once a year. In her most glamorous sari, she had said. How much time would she give me? One evening? Surely I will deserve more, having made the trip all the way from Canada to see her. Well, I shall accept whatever time she gives me with gratitude. Ours will be a spiritual relationship. No sex. She will be wearing a sari, to me a symbol of spiritual beauty. She will grow her hair long again. Hopefully I won't be disturbed by memories of her in Western clothes, in slacks.

Of course my dream entirely depended on Morvarid's declared reluctance to get married to one of her co-religionists. I couldn't carry on a romance, however sublimated, with a married woman. I could very well understand that she, almost a D.Phil. (Oxon.), was not keen to marry a Bombay businessman, least of all one picked for her by her family. But there was no shortage of Indians in Oxford, ever since 1871 when the University had opened its doors to non-members of the Church of England. Not only undergraduates. Also research fellows, visiting professors, even permanent dons. Sometime in 1883 *The Daily Telegraph* had called Oxford 'Benares on the Isis'. With the Parsees forming the most highly educated community in India the number of Parsees among the Indian scholars in Oxford was out of proportion to their number in their home country. Morvarid may not have been interested in a Parsee businessman from Bombay, but a Parsee academic from Oxford would be a different proposition. Was I not being selfish in thinking of my own happiness, rather than hers?

Such were my thoughts as I sat in my Pembroke Street room on that warm Trinity Term evening. It was still bright outside which made me feel even more dejected. I heard light footsteps on the stairs. A woman's footsteps. Probably the girlfriend of one of the undergraduate tenants. But the footsteps stopped just outside my door and I heard two very gentle knocks. Morvarid used to knock at my door this way! Yet I didn't remember Morvarid ever coming to see me so unexpectedly, without giving me a phone call. My heart beating, I opened the door. I saw a slender figure in white sneakers, blue jeans, a red checkered shirt and a red baseball cap. I recognized Joyce. I was disappointed, but not entirely displeased. I was glad to have someone to talk to.

'Come in!' I exclaimed. 'Take a seat.'

She sat on the couch and removed her cap. Her hair, cut short like Morvarid's, had reverted to what I suppose had been its natural dark. Almost, not quite black. Certainly not as black as Morvarid's. I found her even more beautiful with her hair dark. I liked it short. Since Morvarid had cut her hair short I wanted all other women to cut theirs likewise. I noticed her shirt was a man's shirt, the way it was buttoned. No bra of course. Her breasts were swaying freely under her shirt. If her clothes were almost provocatively masculine, she certainly didn't neglect her woman's looks in other, accessory ways. A pair of large earrings hung from her ears. Her lips were of a deep red, much darker than Morvarid's lipstick (when she did use lipstick). Likewise blood-red were her long, sharp finger nails. Her eyes were heavily made up with kohl. Almost Oriental.

'Could I offer you a glass of sherry?' I asked her.

'Not in this heat, thank you. Besides, I am driving,' she answered. 'But if you have cold beer, I would appreciate one.'

'I have Guinness.'

'Great! One bottle of Guinness won't impair my driving. Please, don't look for a glass. I don't mind drinking from the bottle.'

'I am sorry to hear about what has happened to Jack,' I began, not quite sure whether I should say anything. After all the woman was British, and the British do not appreciate having their personal or marital problems mentioned.

'The fool has brought it all upon himself,' she answered, her eyes flashing angrily. 'He wants to divorce me now. Good riddance! He has told me he never really loved me. He treated me like a sex object, not like a woman. He told me he liked me with my hair dyed blonde. Made me look more sexy, he said. So far so good. I loved him, so I was pleased. But then one evening when he was drunk he told me that I was not his love ideal. His ideal of love was an Oriental woman with black hair, so he wanted me to look as different from her as possible.'

'Morvarid?' I asked anxiously. I was truly worried. Never mind the friendship between the two women. But Morvarid was her tenant, and I didn't want her landlady's feminine jealousy to cause problems for her.

'Not so much Morvarid, as what Morvarid represents: the Oriental woman. Well, I am not an Oriental woman, I am an English girl from the Sussex Downs, although I have been told I have some Romany blood in me. That wasn't enough to qualify me for the role, I guess. I don't blame Morvarid in the least. She has never tried to mess it up between us. I don't regret I had invited her to live with us. The break-up of our marriage was inevitable. If Morvarid weren't around he would have found some girl around the Oriental Institute. But she blames herself. I keep telling her not to. Silly girl! She's gone back to wearing a sari. Tells me she will never get married. But don't worry. She will get over it.'

'She has told me she cannot marry me because I am not of her religion,' I said. 'But Jack's, what shall I call it, tragedy has been the catalyst that has made her realize it and forced her to tell me a definite no.'

'I don't know how you are going to resolve your religious differences,' answered Joyce, 'but I know that she loves you.'

'How do you know it?' I exclaimed. 'Has she told you that?'

'No, she hasn't told me,' answered Joyce calmly, 'but it is obvious to me. A woman can see through another woman, even if her race is different. So, you still have your chance, don't lose it! Now, I want to ask you something, Sean. I trust your moral judgment: Jack is offering to leave for me as part of the divorce settlement, the house, the car and half of his money. The house, I need it to live in. Besides, I have put a lot of work into furnishing and decorating it. The car, I need it to move around. Besides, having the car wouldn't do him much good. He's drunk most of the time. I wouldn't care if he smashes himself into a lamppost, but he may run over some innocent pedestrians, some children, God forbid . . . But I am not sure whether I should accept half his money. Sounds so mercenary! I have my scholarship. That's enough for me to live on.'

'You are a woman with dignity, Joyce,' I said, 'but you shouldn't have any qualms about accepting the money. Your scholarship will last only so long as you are a student, while Jack has his don's salary. He has done you a great wrong, but he is honourable enough to be willing to pay for it. Take it, Joyce!'

'Maybe I will in that case,' said Joyce, sounding somewhat pensive. 'But more important: You have called me a woman with dignity. I appreciate that. Now, tell me Sean: Suppose I were unmarried when you had met me and suppose you didn't know Morvarid, would you have considered me for a girlfriend?'

'I certainly would have been tempted to,' I answered in all sincerity. 'You have beauty, not exactly Oriental beauty, but beauty nevertheless, a warm heart, intelligence, a good education, Oxford education, and, yes, sex appeal.' (Absent-mindedly I put my hand on her thigh.)

'You don't find me too androgynous?' she asked me, sounding anxious.

'It is part of your charm. You are an Amazon,' I reassured her. 'I may even, I am not sure, have fallen in love with you. You have impressed me me more than any other Western woman has. But I couldn't have married you. If I did, it would have ended in a tragedy as it has for Jack. And I couldn't in conscience go steady with a girl whom I knew I couldn't marry. At least not for a long time. Joyce, you're a wonderful woman. I hope, I am sure you will meet a man who will love you as you deserve to be loved. But I could never be that man. I am a man possessed, branded with an invisible mark. I am an Orientalist. This in itself doesn't mean anything. The majority of Orientalists marry women of their own race and aren't any less happy for that. Indeed, before the second half of the twentieth century very few Orientalists had Oriental wives. Few Oriental women had any Western education or a chance to meet Western men. I belong to that limited circle of Orientalists who . . . Ever since I was a teenager I knew I had to marry an Oriental girl and I was prepared to search through all the Orient from Morocco to Japan in order to find her. What has made me this way? Maybe it is atavism, the call of some long forgotten Oriental ancestor. Maybe I was married to an Oriental woman (could it have been Morvarid?) in a previous life if we accept the theory of reincarnation. But most likely it was my teenage reading . . . '

'Pierre Loti?' asked Joyce, smiling. I remembered her subject was French literature.

'Pierre Loti and others,' I answered. 'Mostly English authors: Byron and Tom Moore and Disraeli and Rider Haggard and Conrad and James Elroy Flecker. All of them had created some Oriental heroines. Morvarid deals with them in her thesis . . . '

'Yes, I know,' said Joyce. 'I have read her thesis.'

'So,' I continued, 'I have lived as a man lives in a dream. Sometimes I had thought my dream was an illusion and tried to get rid of it by starting an affair with a Canadian or European girl. It always turned sour. When I first met Jack when I came to Oxford as an undergraduate (how many years ago?) I recognized him as a kindred spirit. He was dreaming the same dream. Later he thought he could escape it with your help.'

'The hypocrite! He was using me,' said Joyce with the utmost bitterness.

'He was using you, but he wasn't being a hypocrite,' I answered. 'He sincerely believed you could have had a good marriage, the two of you. Of course he was mistaken. A man like him or me can never have a good marriage except with an Oriental woman.'

'I certainly will not try to draw you out of your Oriental dream,' answered Joyce smiling. 'I know your heart belongs to Morvarid who is my friend, my best friend, and I would never want to mess it up between you and her, but couldn't we also be friends, you and me?'

She put the empty bottle of Guinness on the small table and rose, presumably to leave. I rose also.

'Sure,' I answered. 'I have very much appreciated talking to you, especially now that Morvarid is refusing to see me until she finishes her thesis she says.'

My visitor moved, not towards the door as I expected, but towards my bed. She kicked off her sneakers and threw herself on top of the bed, lying on her back, her hands clasped behind her head. She looked to me like a modern version of Goya's Clothed Maja in blue jeans. Slowly she unbuttoned her man's shirt, half revealing a pair of very feminine breasts. Then she undid the buckle of her belt and opened the zipper of her jeans. I watched, fascinated.

'You can take me if you like' she whispered.

She seemed irresistible. My heart was beating like Great Tom, my physical desire for her was growing big and hard and strong, as big as Tom Tower I thought. Why don't I drive it into her, and drive it into her, and drive it into her, and again, and again, and again until that marvellous moment when all my strength would suddenly vanish and I would fall exhausted upon her bosom and Time would stop. It would stop only for a second, but that second would seem like eternity. I wonder if Einstein hadn't first hit on the idea of relativity of time in the arms of a woman.

Yet I could not do it. I just stood petrified, looking at her, powerless. I felt as if Tom Tower had crumpled down about me.

'Why are you hesitating, Sean?' she asked me in a very gentle voice. 'Is it because I am Jack's wife? Well, I am no longer his wife!' (Her voice changed into a tone almost of anger.) 'If the divorce legalities are taking time, what difference does it make? I know, you Roman Catholics don't believe in divorce, but Jack and I didn't even have an Anglican marriage, just a civil one. Am I still his wife in your eyes? Or are you afraid lest you make me pregnant? Let me reassure you there: I have recently been told by the gynaecologist I cannot bear children because . . . never mind why. I am glad. I wouldn't have wanted to have children with that creep! Would have really complicated matters! I think I understand you, Sean,' she continued in a gentle voice again. 'You are apprehensive lest I hold you to a commitment. I assure you that what I am offering you now I am offering it to you as a free gift, without a string attached. I am a daughter of the sixties, what you used to call a flower child. I don't believe sex should be restricted to marriage. Morvarid thinks so, but that is her culture. We British used to be like that until recently. But we flower children have felt sex is the essence of the joy of life, to be shared with all for whom we have any feelings of friendship and affection. God knows I have been a faithful wife to Jack and I will be a faithful wife to any man I may marry in the future, but now I am a free woman. I see you are longing for Morvarid. She will finish her thesis soon and you will see her. Meanwhile, we could share a little joy together.'

'I do desire you, Joyce.' I said, regaining my composure. 'Very badly. I see the unselfishness of your offer. But I just can't take it. You are telling me you wouldn't hold me to a commitment, but I would feel committed to you even if you disclaim any hold over me. Whatever you would feel about it would be your own business, but for my part it would create a bond between us, stronger than any bond which may exist between me and Morvarid. Oh no, I am not such a good boy. I could seek sexual relief with some sexy woman picked up on Cornmarket, a woman whose name I wouldn't know and whom I would pay afterwards. It would be of no more consequence than getting drunk or smoking a marijuana cigarette. But you are not an anonymous sexy woman. You are Joyce. I know you. I like you. I respect you. I have for you feelings of friendship, even of affection. Precisely because of this I cannot do it with you, Joyce. It would be a betrayal of Morvarid.'

'Oh Sean! You are so idealistic,' said Joyce smiling. 'You really deserve a girl like Morvarid, not a tramp like me!'

She drew up the zipper of her jeans, buckled her belt, buttoned her shirt, sat on the edge of the bed and put on her sneakers. She slowly rose and picked up her cap. Then, all of a sudden, she threw her arms round my neck and kissed me on the lips.

'Good night, Sean! Will see you again soon.'

'You said you were driving. Let me walk with you to your car,' I offered.

'It's very nice of you. You're a real gentleman, Sean. Unlike him,' she answered. I assumed the 'him' referred to her husband (or ex-husband). 'My car is parked on St Aldate's. I hope I don't have a ticket.'

CHAPTER XVI

In spite of myself I felt pleased with the visit. It boosted my male ego. But I was worried. Had Joyce, disappointed by her husband, fallen in love with me, or was she merely behaving in accordance with her hippie philosophy? I hoped it was the latter. I didn't want to hurt her, but, more important, I didn't want her female jealousy to mess it up between Morvarid and me. I didn't look down upon her permissive sexual morality. It wasn't something I would want in a wife, Oriental or otherwise, but who am I to judge other people? I respect people who live up to their principles even when those principles are different from mine. The one thing I cannot stand is hypocrisy. I was sure Joyce lived according to her principles. She believed in the commitment of and the fidelity within marriage, but free sex was OK for an unmarried (or divorced) woman. Anyway, Morvarid knew her and her ideas well, and she accepted her as a friend. That was enough for me.

I hadn't seen Morvarid for weeks. Much, much too long! From time to time I had caught in the distance a glimpse of an orange sari, but I didn't dare to approach, respecting her demand not to try to see her while she was finishing her thesis. Once or twice, unable to restrain myself, I would approach a sari-clad figure only to discover it was a different Indian girl.

One hot afternoon, having lunched in The Roebuck, on my way back to the Bodleian I saw in the north-west corner of

Radcliffe Square, almost under Bishop Heber's oak a slender girl in a blouse of printed cotton showing light green leaves on a dark green background and plain green slacks. On her head she was wearing a wide-brimmed straw hat with a chiffon scarf, also green, tied around it. The end of the scarf, about two feet long, was fluttering in the wind like a pennant. I couldn't see her face because of the shadow cast upon it by her hat. This gave her an air of mystery which drew my attention.

'Sean!' I suddenly heard the familiar and much loved voice. 'At last I am seeing you! I have been trying to phone you for the past two days, but your phone has always been giving the busy signal. Have you been talking to some girl all the time?'

As a matter of fact my telephone had broken down and I was impatiently waiting for it to be repaired. Unfortunately British Telecom was not as quick about it as Bell Canada. Well, maybe in London or Manchester, but not in Oxford.

'Morvarid!' I exclaimed, enraptured by the unexpected friendliness of her greeting. 'Have you finished your thesis?'

'Yes, I handed it in on Tuesday,' answered Morvarid. 'Now I have to sit and wait with my fingers crossed. Elizabeth assures me it is very good and they will have to accept it. If it weren't good she wouldn't have allowed me to present it, she says. But you never know!'

'It is very good! I have read it,' I answered.

'I wish you were my examiner!' she answered, laughing.

'Could I invite you for tea?' I asked her with a slight hesitation.

'Maybe later in the afternoon. It's such a beautiful day! Could we go and sit up there?' She pointed towards Bishop Heber's oak. Of course she did not mean that we should climb up the tree. She wanted us to sit on the mound in Exeter garden overlooking Radcliffe Square. 'Do you remember how we sat there last time?'

'Do I ever remember it!' I exclaimed. 'I remember every word you said. It was a beautiful occasion! I remember you were wearing a green sari.'

'Well, I am wearing green today. You prefer to see me in European clothes, don't you, Sean?'

'I think I do,' I answered with some hesitation. 'You looked lovely, heavenly in a sari, but somehow it has come to symbolize a barrier between us.'

'We shall talk about it when we sit in the garden,' said Morvarid.

We walked down Brasenose Lane, which with the gutter running in the middle of it reminded me of the backlanes of Tehran. The high wall of Exeter garden with the tops of trees showing above it added to the illusion of Iran. We turned right on the Turl and reached the gate of Exeter College. I was no longer feeling self-conscious. By now the porter had come to know me and always greeted me with a friendly 'Good morning' or 'Good afternoon, Sir'. We passed through the gate, crossed the front quadrangle, the dark passage past William Morris Room and found ourselves in the garden. Slowly we crossed the garden and mounted the steps up the mound to the bench under Bishop Heber's oak. Morvarid's green costume blended with the greenness of the garden. She seemed to belong to that garden, like a guardian fairy. A female fairy in a men's college garden? Why not? What do fairies care about University Statutes? They were there long before the University was founded, before the Anglo-Saxon conquest of Britain. They are Celts, like their Irish sisters. Of course I don't believe in fairies. I am an educated man. Contrary to popular misconception we Irish don't believe in fairies. We just know they are there. Sometimes they assume human form. Could Morvarid be a fairy? *Pari* in Persian (pronounced *paree*, entered English and other Western languages in the Turkish form 'peri').

We sat on the bench overlooking Radcliffe Square. Morvarid crossed her trousered legs, took off her hat and laid it on her knee. I couldn't see her eyes because she was wearing dark-green sunglasses. She was wearing lipstick, but, as usual, of a much lighter red than Joyce's. I thought I could discern a pattern there: She wore lipstick only with European clothes, never with a sari. I felt this meeting was a crucial one: It would decide the future of our relationship.

'You have said, Sean, that you felt my sari was inhibiting you, that it was like a barrier between us,' began Morvarid, speaking very slowly. 'I thought I needed such a barrier to protect myself, not just from you, but from all Western men. From all non-Parsee men,' she corrected herself. 'So I went back to wearing a sari, but, after wearing European clothes all these months, I felt very uncomfortable in it. I was longing for the freedom of movement which I had enjoyed in my slacks. But that wasn't all: I discovered I no longer liked the look of myself in a sari. You know the tall mirror in Joyce's sitting-room? I looked into it and I didn't like what I saw. Most of you Western men, especially Orientalists like yourself, find us very glamorous in our saris. But to me it was a raiment of bondage, bondage to a tradition which wouldn't let me live my life the way I wanted and with whom I wanted. I realized I have been in the West too long, I have got myself involved with you too deeply. I can no longer go back to India, I cannot marry a Parsee, or any Indian for that matter, and I can no longer go back to wearing a sari. I had told you last time I thought I was an actress playing the part of a Westernized Indian girl. Maybe

I was in the beginning. But in the end I had really become a Westernized Indian woman. In order to convince my subconscious that there was no going back I decided to get rid of all my saris. I have donated them to the South Asian Women's Mutual Aid Collective in Manchester. Except one, which I have kept as a souvenir and which I may wear just once, for a special occasion, I am not sure.'

'I wish you hadn't given them away!' I couldn't stop myself from exclaiming.

'Sorry, Sean. You must accept me as I am, a Westernized Oriental girl. We discussed it before. You agreed that my giving up the sari was a small enough sacrifice for the sake of our friendship. Just like cutting my hair short.'

I could hardly believe my ears. 'You mean we can be friends like before? You mean,' I hesitated, not certain how to put it, 'you may still consider marrying me?'

'That's what I am telling you, you blockhead!' answered Morvarid, sounding slightly impatient. 'I am telling you I am never going to wear a sari again (except once, and that will be the last time). Those weeks I wasn't seeing you made me sure of how I was feeling about you. Now I can promise you I shall always, always wear European clothes. Am I making myself clear enough?'

I understood that this strange girl was using the metaphor of wearing European clothes to signify her acceptance of my proposal, of my insistence to marry her. I threw my arm round her shoulder, drew her towards me and kissed her on the lips.

'Not here, Sean,' she whispered. 'People are watching us.'

'They cannot see us up here' I answered. From where we were sitting we could see the crowds of undergraduates and tourists on Radcliffe Square, but it would have been difficult for them to see us.

'You are going to crumple my hat,' said Morvarid. Her voice sounded severe, but her lips were smiling. 'Sit up straight. I haven't finished talking. Joyce has told me you refused the consolation she was offering you because of, as you had explained it to her, your commitment to me in spite of what I thought was my final no to your proposal. I was deeply moved.'

'I must tell you the truth,' I said, gearing myself for the consequences. 'It wasn't virtue on my part, it was weakness. I was physically unable to do it. But, yes, it was the apprehension of betraying you which had inhibited me.'

'I still appreciate the fact that you didn't give in,' answered Morvarid. 'But,' she continued, 'I was feeling guilty about what had happened to Jack. You Catholics have an interesting practice which helps you to get rid of your guilt feelings: confession. Why don't I try it, I thought. I was feeling so desperate I was ready to try anything. So I went to see Father Pereira and told him I would like to make a confession to him.'

'Oh yes,' I interjected. 'He had extracted a confession from me when I was sick. I think I had told you about it. He had told me I shouldn't feel guilty about desiring you since I am determined to marry you.'

'Good for you,' answered Morvarid, 'but my problem was more complicated. Father Pereira told me I didn't have to make a confession. All my sins could be washed clean by baptism. I told him I wasn't ready for baptism yet, but I still wanted to talk to him. He told me that Jack's misfortune was not my fault and that I shouldn't feel guilty about it. I should just pray for him. Christian prayer or Zoroastrian prayer, doesn't matter. I felt a tremendous sense of relief. He has a very high opinion of you. Maybe I shall get baptized after all. I would rather be a good Catholic than a bad Zoroastrian who has married outside her faith. After all there are more Catholics than Zoroastrians in India.'

'So! Let us get married as soon as possible!' I exclaimed. I was thinking of the limited time I had left in Oxford before I would have to return to McGill for the beginning of the academic year.

'Let us wait until I get my D.Phil.' answered Morvarid, obviously amused by my impatience. 'Suppose my thesis is not accepted and I have to rewrite it, completely or some chapters? I don't want to get married until I have finished with it once and for all.'

CHAPTER XVII

To take Morvarid's mind off her thesis I suggested a short trip away from Oxford. London? she proposed. No, I said firmly. In London she would be reminded of it by the libraries, by her acquaintances at London University. Let us go to a more quiet place without academic reminders. Joyce suggested Brighton. She herself was a native of Rottingdean, a picturesque village four miles East of Brighton, at one time a centre of smuggling. She was very proud of her smuggler ancestors, the 'gentlemen' celebrated by Kipling. Morvarid accepted the suggestion on the condition that we would book two separate hotel rooms.

The main attraction of Brighton is of course the beach, but Morvarid was not much impressed. She couldn't swim and she wasn't very interested to learn when I offered to teach her. As to lying in the sun, as most women like to do, the prospect did not appeal to her at all.

'I think I am dark enough for your Orientalist taste,' she said laughing. 'If I lie in the sun I shall become black like a Malayali Christian from Kerala!'

Actually she took great care to protect herself from the sun, even the English sun, by wearing loose-fitting long-sleeved blouses, white cotton slacks, a wide-brimmed straw hat and a pair of dark glasses. The dark glasses and the shade cast upon her face by the brim of her hat gave her that mysterious look which I always found exciting.

'Brighton beach isn't so pleasant with its hard, sharp stones,'

I told her. 'One day I shall take you to Florya. Beautiful golden sand and warm water.'

'Where is Florya? in Florida?'

'In Turkey, on the Marmara Sea, near Istanbul.'

It being Brighton, not Florya, we spent little time on the seaside. We explored the Lanes, a small labyrinth of narrow streets, full of boutiques, with overhanging upper stories. Reminded me of old towns in Turkey. Pedestrians only. No cars. I hate cars. Morvarid loved the fashion boutiques and shoe shops, but when I found an antiquarian bookshop in Meeting House Lane she grabbed me by the hand and dragged me away. We took most of our meals in the picturesque cafes in the Lanes. Slightly exotic, almost Mediterranean, certainly un-English cuisine.

I was of course most interested in the Oriental, or rather Orientalist heritage of Brighton. There was the Prince Regent's Royal Pavilion, a strange building with a tea trade Chinese interior, and, nearer to my Orient, an Indo-Islamic façade with onion domes and thin minarets. Morvarid did not appreciate the building:

'It is a grotesque parody of Indian architecture! We have some ugly buildings in Bombay, but this one beats them all. Even the craziest and most extravagant maharaja wouldn't have built something like this.'

I tended to agree with her. It was a lack of proportion between various elements of the building that gave it its incongruous look. Sure, John Nash was a great architect, but he just couldn't grasp the spirit of Islamic architecture. And yet, there was something in the building which appealed to my imagination. It represented an Orientalist dream, ignorant of the real Orient, yet longing for it. I shared this thought with Morvarid, but she was not impressed:

'It looks like a European woman trying to wear a sari,' she

said in a sarcastic tone. 'Joyce had once borrowed one of my saris to go to a party. She looked just as grotesque.'

Yet just across a small park, facing the Pavilion stands a building which we found both more dignified and more genuinely Oriental: the Dome Theatre, originally built as the Royal Stables by William Porden, an architect now almost forgotten, but with a much greater feeling for Islamic style than his more famous colleague, John Nash. Seldom have horses had such a palatial residence. It is supposed to be inspired by the Jami' Masjid or the Great Mosque of Delhi. Morvarid reluctantly agreed:

'I have seen the Jami' Masjid, although I haven't been inside it.' (The Zoroastrians, like the Oriental Christians, are very reluctant to enter mosques, even when those mosques are tourist attractions, welcoming non-Muslim visitors.) 'It is a rather poor imitation, but it has some similarities. See those arches over there?'

Too bad the Dome has been eclipsed by the Pavilion which has become almost a symbol of Brighton! Yet the Royal Pavilion with its phoney Chinese interior and equally phoney Indo-Islamic façade did have a genuine Indian past, as Morvarid would remind me: During World War I it was used as a hospital for wounded Indian soldiers. Morvarid's great-uncle, Dr Meherbakhsh Cama had been a surgeon in the British Indian Army during World War I.

'He was taking care of all wounded, Indian, British, even German POWs without distinction,' she was telling me proudly. 'He was stationed here for some time. After the War he was given an OBE by George V, but returned it as a protest after the Amritsar Massacre. I remember him dimly as a very, very old man with a long white beard. He always used to give me candies.'

To Morvarid then the Royal Pavilion was a place of pilgrimage, even though she didn't appreciate its architecture.

But she was most anxious to return to Oxford to learn whether her thesis had been accepted.

CHAPTER XVIII

Morvarid's apprehensions had proved groundless. Her thesis was not only accepted, but strongly praised by the examiners. It was recommended for publication with the proviso that some minor mistakes in the bibliography should be corrected in the printed version. There were several Indian girls taking their degrees at the same time as Morvarid. In accordance with the regulations governing academic dress they wore black saris over white blouses, but my fiancée, as she now was, wore a black jacket and skirt like all the other women degree recipients. I thought she looked very chic, much more elegant than her countrywomen. Sure, I appreciate beautiful women in saris, but not in black saris. Silly girls! They could have worn a black jacket and skirt just for this occasion.

Soon afterwards we were married by Father Pereira in the Catholic Chaplaincy, popularly referred to as the Newman Chapel. Morvarid arrived, wearing, as promised, her red sari with the gold-embroidered border. The end of the sari covered her head, scarcely leaving the face to be seen. She looked absolutely beautiful, the way she had appeared to me before she began wearing European clothes. It was that ethereal sort of beauty, too sacred to provoke a sensual thought. Amazing how a woman's personality can change with a change of dress! I rushed to embrace her.

'A little patience, Sean,' she whispered. 'I am not your wife yet.' She pointed to her sari. I noticed she was wearing lipstick, the only time I remember seeing her wearing lipstick with a sari.

Father Pereira was supposed to meet us at the entrance to the chapel but he was nowhere to be seen. We weren't going to wait for him outside. I took my bride by the hand and led her in. We marched down the aisle towards the altar. I liked it that way. I don't like the custom of the bride having to be 'given away' by her father, big brother or some other male member of the family, even if it is only a formality. I was a free man marrying a free woman! Father Pereira appeared at the altar, we both said 'Yes, I will' and he pronounced us man and wife. The long wait was over.

As we were leaving the chapel an uninvited, but not unwelcome, photographer from the *Oxford Mail* took our picture. That photo appeared in the social gossip section of the paper with the caption: 'Oxford beauty weds Canadian prof.' I was hoping Jack would not see that particular issue of *Oxford Mail*.'

'I really look like a respectable Parsee bride,' Morvarid commented about the picture sometime later. 'I can send it to my family at home. Even you look dark enough to pass for a Parsee.'

'Must be my Cree blood,' I answered.

Of course she was joking. She couldn't hide the fact that she had married outside her religion.

We had a small reception arranged by Joyce in her house which was going to be Morvarid's and my home for the short time remaining to us in Oxford before our departure for Canada. Almost all the guests were Morvarid's friends and I had met most of them. Most of them were women. Joyce was, as usual, a charming hostess. I found a sad irony in the fact that our wedding party was being hosted by a divorced woman in what had until recently been the home of her husband who had been my friend, at one time my best friend. Of course he was absent but his shadow was there. I didn't say a word about this to Morvarid, but no doubt she could feel it too, probably stronger than me.

I was expecting Morvarid to remain in her red sari till the end of the party. However, almost as soon as we arrived, she ran upstairs and reappeared a few minutes later wearing a green trouser suit with a white lacy blouse. The guests must have been impressed by the transformation because they broke into applause. The women crowded round her admiring her costume. For a fraction of a second I felt somewhat sad. I knew I would never see her in a sari again. I was hoping to see her in her sari for an hour or two longer. Yet almost immediately my sadness was overcome by an immense sense of joy. Only now it dawned upon my subconscious that Morvarid was indeed my wife. Tonight ...

CHAPTER XIX

Warneford Hospital, originally called the Oxford Lunatic Asylum, has played host to more members of the University, undergraduates and dons, than is generally acknowledged. Only the sturdy Oxford townsfolk, those whose ancestors used to drive oxen across the Isis long before the University was even thought of, would shrug their shoulders and express no surprise. They knew that most, if not all, wearers of gowns were at least a little mad. The Warneford was the right place for them.

I was on my way to visit one of those patients from the University, Jack Curtis from Jesus College and the Oriental Institute. I felt that, whatever had happened between us, I just couldn't leave Oxford and go back to Canada without saying farewell to my once best friend. Morvarid was not with me. We had both agreed that her coming to visit him with me now that she was my wife would have been too insensitive. I didn't know how I would be received myself, but I felt I had to make the gesture.

A psychiatric hospital used to conjure up visions of prison-like structures which would drive the inmates even more crazy than they actually were. This may have been true in the 18th century. The Warneford however, opened in 1826, looks more like a Victorian country hotel set in a large green park. I found myself in front of a desk with a sign saying INFORMATION above it.

'Good afternoon, Miss. I should like to see one of the

patients, Mr Jack Curtis.' (I had called him Mr, not Dr Curtis, not to deny his well-earned D.Phil., but in hospital surroundings the title 'Doctor' always denotes a member of the staff.)

'What is your name, Sir?' asked the girl.

'Sean O'Malley.'

The girl picked up a telephone receiver and dialled a number:

'Mr Curtis? There is a gentleman wishing to see you, Sir. Mr Sean O'Malley. Shall I send him to your ward or will you come down to the lobby to meet him?'

I couldn't hear the answer, but I saw a cloud coming over her face. She lay down the receiver.

'I am sorry, Sir, but Mr Curtis tells me he does not wish to receive any visitors today.'

I suspect it was her tactful British way of telling me that Mr Curtis did not wish to see this particular visitor.

At that moment a short, rather fat man with greying hair surrounding a bald area who had been looking at a notice board with a sign saying STAFF NOTICES sharply turned round and walked towards me. He had a high forehead usually attributed to intellectuals and slightly Middle Eastern features: a large aquiline nose and arched black eyebrows. He looked like an Arab or an Armenian, I thought.

'Professor O'Malley?' he asked stretching out his hand. 'I am Dr Harry Solomon, Mr Curtis's therapist. I think I saw you at Radcliffe Infirmary when you came to visit Mr Curtis. And of course I saw your photograph in the *Oxford Mail* with your beautiful bride. I am sorry Mr Curtis is refusing to see you, but I am sure you can understand the circumstances and forgive him.'

In spite of his Middle Eastern features his English showed no trace of Arabic or any other foreign accent. It wasn't the fastidious Oxford English though. It was very much London English with a very slight trace of East End Cockney.

'Yes, I understand,' I replied. 'I would probably have reacted the same in his situation.'

Actually I wasn't altogether displeased at Jack's refusal to see me. I was feeling very nervous about presenting myself before him as the husband of the woman he loved. Well, I have done my gesture of goodwill. I felt relieved.

'Could I invite you for a cup of tea in my office?' asked Dr Solomon. 'No doubt you would like to have some information about your friend's condition. Also, if you would allow me, I would permit myself to ask you a few questions. My patient has told me a lot about you, and if I see your point of view it will help me to diagnose his state more exactly. Of course you are in no way obligated,' he added anxiously.

'I shall be very pleased to have a talk with you, Doctor, although I am sure you are a very busy man,' I replied.

He led me into what looked like a regular doctor's office occupied by a large desk with neatly arranged piles of papers on it. How unlike the desks of most academics, including myself, I thought. There was a revolving chair behind the desk and a very comfortable-looking armchair in front of it. The walls of the room were lined with books. The only object not usually found in most doctors' offices was a reclining couch a little further from the desk.

'Please make yourself comfortable,' said the doctor, 'on the chair or on the couch, whichever you prefer.'

'I am not exactly your patient,' I said, self-consciously seating myself in the armchair.

Dr Solomon smiled: 'Most of my patients prefer to sit on the chair. I am keeping the couch mainly for tradition's sake. Do you take milk with your tea, Professor O'Malley?'

He walked towards a small table in the corner of the room on which stood an electric kettle, a small clay teapot and two cups.

'Excuse me for a moment, I must go and bring some milk.'

'Please, Doctor,' I stopped him. 'I usually drink tea without milk, the Iranian way. Unless of course you want milk for yourself.'

'I cannot take milk just now because I had meat for lunch,' explained the doctor, switching on the electric kettle.

'Do you offer tea to your patients, Doctor?' I asked.

'Oh yes!' he answered, smiling. 'Makes them feel relaxed and less inhibited to talk.'

He walked towards a filing cabinet and took out a file. I assumed it was patient Jack Curtis's file. He sat behind the desk and put on a pair of horn-rimmed glasses.

'So, let me explain to you Mr Curtis's state of health as briefly as I can,' he began, looking at the file. 'My colleagues in Radcliffe Infirmary have succeeded in completely purging him from the effects of the drugs he had taken, so his physical health is back to normal. Regarding his mental health let me assure you that he is not insane in a clinical sense. His mind is as rational as yours or mine. Legally he can conduct his divorce case and dispose of his property and finances in any way he wishes. He does however suffer from a very acute depression which drives him to seek refuge in alcohol which is bad enough and in under-the-counter drugs which is much more dangerous. I am giving him a few anti-depressant drugs, but those give him only a partial and temporary relief. The cause of his depression is psychological, not physical. My aim is to remove that cause by trying to convince him to change his attitude. That I can do only by persuasion.'

The water had come to a boil. The doctor got up and made the tea.

'You say you are trying to convince him to change his attitude. His attitude towards what? I do not understand,' I asked. I was puzzled.

'The trouble with him is that he is romantic,' said the doctor. 'And that is very bad, very bad.'

I had heard these words somewhere, but where? I couldn't remember. Oh yes! I remembered suddenly: These were the very words used by Stein, an amateur psychoanalyst but a very wise man in his analysis of Lord Jim in Conrad's novel. Yet Stein had immediately followed his statement by its exact opposite, 'Very good, too'. I sat in silence waiting for the doctor to say something to that effect. But no 'Very good, too' or anything like it came.

'Is being romantic so bad?' I asked in order to break the silence. 'Ever since I was a teenager I had thought of myself as a romantic.'

'And do you still think of yourself as such?' asked the doctor.

'I would say yes,' I answered.

'Please do not get me wrong,' said the doctor. 'I am fully aware of the contribution of romanticism to literature and art and music. I love the music of Chopin and Liszt. But what I find most pernicious is the myth of romantic love. Sure, it has inspired some of the world's greatest poetry, but the harm it has done to our mental health is beyond measure.'

'Is sexual attraction then the only thing there is to love?' I asked in surprise.

'In a healthy individual, yes,' answered the doctor. 'I do not deny the power of romantic love so-called. But it is a noxious power. It is a neurosis grown out of repressed sexuality. Our aim is to make the patient aware of what it really is and to liberate him from it.'

'Then would you make sexual attraction the only basis for marriage?' I asked incredulously.

'Certainly not!' answered the doctor with emphasis. 'Sex is a necessary element in a harmonious marriage, but there are many other factors to be considered, such as a compatible temperament, family considerations, the man's capacities as provider, the woman's capacities as homemaker... Now romantic love, what we call falling in love, blinds the lover to all these practical but necessary considerations. It is a form of madness.'

'What you are telling me, Doctor, makes me afraid for the future of my own marriage,' I said. I was smiling, but feeling uneasy inside. 'I fell in love with my wife when I met her and I am still in love with her. It wasn't just sex. It was something I find it most difficult to describe. I had always had a dream, call it an obsession if you like, of marrying a woman from the Orient. And in her I found the ideal I was looking for.'

I noticed the doctor was paying a very close attention to my words and quickly writing something with a sharp pencil. I suspected he was taking down my words in a form of shorthand.

'You are not my patient, Professor O'Malley, and I don't know all the circumstances of your marriage,' he said. 'But I may have overstated my case. A marriage based on romantic love is not necessarily bound to failure if it contains other, more positive elements. You are a university professor. I believe your wife has recently earned a D.Phil. Your minds may be very compatible with each other and your marriage may turn out to be very happy in spite of, not because of, the romantic aura you have surrounded it. I certainly wish you all happiness. Now to come to your friend: I shall try to be as brief as I can and to avoid professional jargon.'

He glanced at the open file.

'Mr Curtis had been carrying within him, since he was a teenager the image of an ideal woman, what Carl Jung would have called his "anima". I am not a Jungian, mind you. I believe Jung has greatly distorted Freud's psychoanalysis with his superstitions . . . '

'Like astrology?' I asked.

'Astrology, alchemy, synchronicity . . . ' answered Dr Solomon, sounding slightly annoyed at my interruption. 'But nevertheless he has made some very important contributions to psychology. The anima archetype is one of those. The image of the woman may vary from man to man, but the psychological mechanism is the same. In Mr Curtis's case that woman had to be an Oriental woman. Have you by any chance read Rider Haggard's *She*?'

'Of course.'

'Haggard has been dismissed by most literary critics as a writer of adventure stories for boys, and indeed, most of his novels are little more than adventure stories for boys. But he has produced some works of real power. Among those *She* stands out as a great book. She, Ayesha, is the expression of Haggard's anima, perhaps the greatest expression of an author's anima in all literature.'

'Yes' I said. 'I know Haggard has been appreciated by psychologists, by Freud and Jung more than by literary critics. My wife has a chapter about Ayesha in her thesis about the treatment of the Oriental woman in English literature.'

'Indeed?' exclaimed the doctor. 'I must read it! Now my patient has been obsessed with the image of his Oriental woman just as Leo Vincey/Rider Haggard had been obsessed with his dream of Ayesha.'

'Just like me!' I exclaimed. 'This was what drew us together when we were undergraduates!'

'When Mr Curtis met Miss M.C. . . . ' continued the doctor.

'Miss M.C.? I was puzzled for a moment. 'Of course! Morvarid Cama!'

'In order to protect the privacy of various persons mentioned by our patients we note only their initials in our records,' explained the doctor. 'Thus you are referred to as S.O. So, when Mr Curtis met Miss M.C. he thought he saw in her his ideal Oriental woman and fell in love with her. He claims there was no sexual attraction in his love for her, but we know that all so-called romantic love is nothing more than a sublimation of repressed sexuality. He proposed marriage to her. Because of her religion she was most hesitant to accept. (I understand her very well, since I myself belong to a religious tradition which does not permit intermarriage, although in this secular age how many of our young people care?) She introduced him to her friend Miss J.S.' (Joyce Savage of course, I remembered Joyce's maiden name) 'and encouraged him to take a serious interest in her. Mr Curtis found Miss J.S. most attractive sexually, renounced his Oriental dream and married her. On the face of it he did the wise thing. By itself sexual attraction is not enough for a successful marriage, but it is one of its most necessary components. Unlike romantic love which is, as I have pointed out to you, more of a liability than an asset. Yet the marriage was bound to failure because Mr Curtis, in his subconscious, continued to be in love with Miss M.C. and the Oriental dream she represented. Rather foolishly Mrs Curtis invited Miss M.C. to become her tenant. Equally foolishly Miss M.C. accepted. Mr Curtis was more pleased with the situation than he would have admitted to himself. Until S.O., that is yourself, Sir, arrived on the scene. Miss M.C. began regularly seeing S.O. and told the Curtises she was seriously considering marrying him. Mr Curtis was shocked to learn that she would after all sacrifice her religion for the sake of another man. She was not unobtainable after all. He felt he had thrown away his chance when he decided to marry Miss J.S. Also, at about the same time as she began to date S.O., Miss M.C. began to dress in a way Mr Curtis found more stimulating sexually. He felt he had made a terrible mistake in marrying Miss J.S. He told Miss M.C. he still loved her, would divorce his wife and begged her, Miss M.C. to marry him. Miss M.C. not only refused, but was shocked and frightened. It was then that Mr Curtis left home and went to the Hideaway Hotel.' The doctor paused.

'You have invited me, Doctor, to act as a sort of witness,' I said. 'I can assure you that the facts as you have related them, no doubt obtained from the patient, are correct. As to your interpretation it would be most arrogant for me, a layman, to dispute it. But, may I ask, what remedy do you propose for my friend? I sure don't want him to continue loving my wife. Could some other Oriental woman take her place as his Oriental anima?'

'By all means,' answered the doctor. 'The sooner he meets a compatible woman the better. Her nationality, whether she is Oriental or not, doesn't matter. What matters is that he must not see his anima in her, or, to put it in plain language, he must not fall in love with her or he will be faced with the same problem again, and very likely it will destroy him.'

'I do not understand you, Doctor,' I said. 'You have expressed an admiration for Rider Haggard's *She* as the supreme example of an author's yearning for his anima. Yet now you are condemning it. Forgive my layman's ignorance, but I see a contradiction here.'

'I do not deny the power of romantic love, of the anima,' answered the doctor, 'and, like so many of my colleagues, I admire Haggard's presentation of it. What I object to is the theory, first put forward by the Provençal troubadours (who may have got the idea from the Arabs, you know better than me) and developed to the full by the romantic poets, that this force is something positive. Jung himself claimed so, but Jung was wrong about so many things . . . Now, coming back to Haggard's *She*: How does Leo Vincey's quest end? With Ayesha's death when her two thousand plus years catch up with her. Then, have you read its sequel, *Ayesha, the Return of She*?'

'Oh yes, I was so fascinated by *She* that I was most eager to read the sequel,' I answered.

'So, if you remember, Leo Vincey, guided by little else than intuition, travels to Tibet in the sure hope of finding Ayesha there. And, indeed he does find her there, reincarnated or resurrected. When, at last he obtains his ultimate desire and kisses her lips, he drops dead. Of course the kiss here is a Victorian euphemism for sexual intercourse. In his subconscious Haggard knew that romantic love is something deadly. Now my task is to liberate my patient from his romantic obsession, so that hopefully he may make a mature decision in the choice of a future marriage partner.'

The conversation had left me bewildered. I had read a few books on psychology, but could hardly claim to be an expert on the subject. I was pleased the doctor was trying to cure Jack of his intense love for Morvarid, but I felt most apprehensive about his aim to demolish the very notion of love and reduce it to mere sexual attraction. The romantic in me rebelled against it. The doctor claimed to be a realist. He acknowledged the power of emotion, of love, but regarded it as something evil, to be destroyed. Then it occurred to me: His intense hatred of romantic love was very similar to the 'Christian' puritan's hatred of sex, and just as irrational. It was not in his patient that he wanted to kill the longing for the anima, but in himself. Something terribly painful must have happened in his experience.

'Are you married, Doctor?' I asked him suddenly.

'Alas, my dear Sir,' he answered sadly. 'I am divorced. My wife was a medical doctor and a member of my community' (I assumed he meant his ethno-religious community), 'but, nevertheless . . . ' His voice seemed to fade.

On my return to Joyce's home I related the visit to Joyce and Morvarid. Joyce shrugged her shoulders:

'You didn't miss much if you failed to see him,' (meaning of course Jack). 'The bum did one wise thing if he refused to see you. Well, I shouldn't be vindictive. I hope the Jewish shrink cures him and lets him out soon.'

Morvarid sat silent in her friend's presence But in the privacy of our bedroom she burst into tears: 'Oh Sean! Let us get away from here and go to Canada as soon as we can!'

I assured her that indeed we could leave for Canada soon, maybe within 10 days, or two weeks. She calmed down and smiled.

'Tomorrow,' she said, 'if the weather is nice, let us take a long walk round Oxford. We shall walk by the river. Then we shall come back to town and sit in Exeter garden facing the Camera. My most beautiful memories are from that garden. Then we shall have dinner at the Taj Mahal.'

I understood that this was going to be her farewell to Oxford. She didn't expect to see Oxford again.

EPILOGUE

As I had predicted, Dr Morvarid Cama O'Malley with her Oxford D.Phil. was 'grabbed' by McGill's English Department. She proposed to teach a course on 'The History of Anglo-Indian Literature' which would include all British writings about India, beginning with the 14th century epic *King Alisaunder* about Alexander's victory over King Porus in the Punjab, and all the writings in the English language produced by Indians from the early 19th century onwards. A body of literature more voluminous than Canadian literature in English. With the rising interest in the Third World her course immediately became immensely popular with McGill students. Two years later her thesis on *The Portrayal of the Oriental Woman in Romantic and Victorian Literature* was published by Oxford University Press. The book received enthusiastic reviews in literary journals. Only Edmund Saad, writing in the *New York Review of Books*, took her to task for failing to point out how British authors, in their stereotyping of the Oriental woman had, consciously or otherwise, helped the cause of Western imperialism. My own sabbatical study, *The History of Persian Studies in Oxford* was likewise published by OUP. Of course only Orientalists found it of any interest.

On Morvarid's insistence we bought a house in Notre-Dame-de-Grâce district of Montreal. With my nomadic background I was at first very opposed to the idea of buying a house, but when I saw the inside of the building with its panelled walls reminding me of Oxford colleges I gave in. Morvarid decorated the house to give it an Oriental atmosphere.

I didn't learn much Gujarati from her except the alphabet and a few words. I thought we would make a trip to India to visit her family in Bombay, but she stubbornly opposed it:

'If they want to see me let them come and visit us here. I am not going. You go by yourself if you like.'

I didn't feel like going to India without her. Likewise she was reluctant to revisit England:

'I wouldn't mind seeing London again, the museums, the theatres, the shops. But it would be so hard to go to London and not to go to Oxford, at least for the day.'

Self-exiled from the two countries in which she had spent her childhood and youth Morvarid slowly became Canadianized, at least superficially. She improved her French (mainly in order to enjoy the French theatre of Montreal), but never learned to understand *joual*, the French-Canadian equivalent of Cockney. Gradually she gave up doing reSEARCH at McGill. She began to do REsearch instead. Less and less often she would wear a trouser suit. More and more often she would wear a pant suit. Eventually she would wear pants all the time as Canadian women do. Dresses and skirts were phased out of her attire so gradually I hardly became aware of it. I wonder if she was consciously aware of it herself. Very different from her dramatic rejection of the sari. Actually she wasn't being different from other (East) Indian women in Canada. They seldom wear the sari here as they do in England. No doubt the climate has to do with it. But perhaps there are some deeper psychosocial reasons for it? Whatever the reason, all of Morvarid's Montreal Indian friends have exchanged their saris for slacks or jeans. Morvarid strongly approves. Since she had felt compelled to give up the sari herself she instinctively would like all other Indian women to do likewise.

Yet, however Canadianized she may have become in dress and speech, she never came to understand the ruthless competition of the Canadian workplace. In spite of her academic success she never rose to a rank higher than an assistant professor. She never was ambitious about power, so she didn't care.

For several years Morvarid and Joyce wrote each other long letters. Joyce was not permitted to transfer to Advanced Student status and present her thesis for a D.Phil., but she was given a B.Litt., corresponding to MA. in other universities. Her thesis about George Sand was published by Virago Press in London. Soon after her divorce became final she married a history don from Balliol. We invited her and her new husband to visit us in Montreal. She wrote they may come 'next summer' which again became 'next summer' when next summer came, and 'next summer' again. Gradually the correspondence became less frequent, then it stopped altogether.

In her letters Joyce never mentioned Jack, and of course we didn't expect her to tell us about her ex-husband about whom she was understandably bitter. We did get some news about him from Morvarid's many other friends in Oxford. At the end of summer Jack left the hospital in time to resume his teaching at the Oriental Institute. However he wasn't as successful a tutor as before. He was constantly being warned about his drunkenness. Now heavy drinking, by dons and undergraduates alike, is a time-honoured Oxford tradition, but it must not affect one's ability to teach or study. It is perfectly all right for a don to get drunk every evening, as long as he is sober enough to conduct his tutorial the following morning. Apparently Dr Curtis was not always sober enough. One morning during Trinity Term, after a disciplinary session with the Director of the Institute, he stormed out of the latter's office, slamming the door behind him. No one knew for certain what had gone on behind the closed door, but a secretary had told her best friend, on condition of the strictest secrecy, that Dr Curtis had shouted at the Director 'You miserable little shit!' The friend told another friend, in the strictest secrecy of course, and soon all Oxford was gossiping about the incident with appropriate expressions of horror. That was the end of Dr Curtis's Oxford career.

Nobody knew what happened to him afterwards. According to one version he accepted a teaching position at a university in Australia, according to another he joined the British Council as a teacher of English abroad. Later on there came rumours that he had been seen in a pot-smoking commune in San Francisco. Some said he had joined Rev. Jim Jones's sect and gone off to Guiana with him. However his body was not found after the mass suicide in Jonestown. But others said that he had never left England at all, but, like another Oxford scholar before him, joined a Gipsy band

> 'And roamed the world with that wild brotherhood,
> And came, as most men deemed, to little good,
> But came to Oxford and his friends no more.'

'Maybe he will at last find a woman who will fulfil his Oriental dream' I said to Morvarid. 'After all the Gipsies come from India. They still speak an Indian language.'

My own Oriental dream woman looked sceptical. 'What will he find? An illiterate Gipsy?' she asked, twisting her mouth.

I wrote to Dr Solomon expressing my anxiety about my once best friend. He replied that, sorry, he did not know Mr Curtis's whereabouts, but even if he did he would not have been able to tell me because the Hospital's code of ethics strictly forbade giving any information about former patients.

The break between Jack and me, inevitable though it was, was truly painful to me. He has been the indirect cause of the impossibility of my ever seeing Oxford again. I had pointed out to Morvarid that there was nothing for her to fear in Oxford any more. Jack was no longer there, and we didn't know where he was. Indeed, we didn't even know whether he was dead or alive. It made no difference, she answered. Dead or alive, his memories were haunting Oxford like a ghost, and she couldn't face them. And I don't feel like going to Oxford, even for a short visit, without her.